A COMPANY AFFAIR

When Francesca Lorrimer's father dies, she is determined to continue running his engineering business alone. The good-looking and charming Howard Rutherford, Managing Director of a large, local company, offers help and a merger deal. He appears to accept her refusal, but there is someone wanting to destroy Lorrimers and ruin Francesca. Is Howard really as straightforward as he seems? Francesca has reason for doubts, but she is also falling in love with him . . .

ELIZABETH STEVENS

A COMPANY AFFAIR

Complete and Unabridged

LINFORD
Leicester

First Linford Edition
published 1997

British Library CIP Data

Stevens, Elizabeth
    A company affair.—Large print ed.—
Linford romance library
1. Love stories
2. Large type books
I. Title
823.9′14 [F]

ISBN 0–7089–5086–8

Published by
F. A. Thorpe (Publishing) Ltd.
Anstey, Leicestershire

Set by Words & Graphics Ltd.
Anstey, Leicestershire
Printed and bound in Great Britain by
T. J. International Ltd., Padstow, Cornwall

This book is printed on acid-free paper

1

FRANCESCA LORRIMER picked up the letter from a pile on her desk, frowning as she read it. It seemed that the parts ordered by Wentworth Engineering Company had not arrived on time, as promised. The letter pointed out that this order was needed urgently, with a hint that if Lorrimers could not supply within the next twenty-four hours, the order must be placed elsewhere.

"That's strange; I'm sure this was dealt with more than a week ago," she muttered. "We can't risk losing them. The order isn't a big one but Wentworths are regular customers." She would investigate what had happened, straight away, then telephone Wentworths and apologise. She rose from her chair, letter in hand, and was about to cross the passage to her secretary's office, where the files were kept, when she became aware of someone standing in the doorway, blocking her exit. He must have been standing there for at least a couple of minutes, watching her. She looked up sharply. The man was a stranger, not anyone on the staff.

"Who are you? What do you want? What are you doing here?" She demanded. "How did you get into my office? Don't you know you're supposed to report to Reception first?"

"What a lot of questions! Which am I to answer first?" He smiled lazily at her, eyeing her up and down. She found the action irritatingly sexist, and glared at him. Somehow, it was even more annoying because he was rather good-looking; tall, with thick, dark hair, brown eyes and clean shaven, with smooth, tanned skin. He was probably a salesman, slipping past the girl in the outer office to come and try to interest her in some kind of goods or services she did not want or need. Lorrimers had their share of such opportunists and she really had no time to waste on one of them this morning.

"Do you realise you are trespassing? You should have reported to the person in Reception. Didn't you read the notice?" Francesca's tone implied, couldn't he read? And she was gratified to see he looked slightly abashed.

"I'm sorry. I did wait in Reception but there was no one around, so I thought I might as well come and find you myself."

Mentally, Francesca kicked herself. Sally, the girl who should have been there, must be having her coffee break, and Mavis, who would have relieved her had anyone been expected, was typing letters in the other office, too busy to man reception on the off-chance of an unexpected caller. It would have to have been just the time this creature chose to arrive! Well, she'd despatch him right away; she didn't have time to waste listening to his sales pitch.

"I'm sorry about that. But I'm afraid you've had a wasted journey. I really don't have time to hear what you're selling, and in any case, I doubt if I would be interested — "

"Oh, I'm not selling." The lazy smile took in her annoyance with an amused glance. "But I think you will be interested in what I'm offering, all the same, Miss Lorrimer."

"I doubt it. If you didn't have an appointment then I'm afraid it's impossible for me to spare you any time, Mr — ?" Francesca picked up another letter, pointedly.

"My name's Howard Rutherford. And I'm not selling anything. I'm interested in buying," he said.

"What?" Francesca's head shot up, her light brown hair bouncing on her shoulders. Rutherfords was the largest engineering company in the area, and Howard Rutherford was their Managing Director. She knew the name well enough, though she had never met this man before. And Rutherfords were

4

Lorrimer's biggest customer.

"I'm sorry! I didn't realise who you were!" She exclaimed, embarrassed. What had she said, she thought anxiously. Even if not actually rude, she'd certainly been very sharp and off-hand.

Howard came fully into the small office, and his large frame seemed to dominate the room. He dropped his bantering manner as he said, "Miss Lorrimer, may I offer you my most sincere condolences? I was so very sorry to hear of your father's death."

"Thank you. It was rather a shock to us all. He died so suddenly and completely unexpectedly," Francesca replied.

"The whole town was saddened to hear about it. Your father was well liked in the community. You must be finding things very difficult without him."

"Well, I miss him, of course. It's nearly a month since he died but I still find myself forgetting he's no longer here." Francesca stopped. She didn't want to talk to this man about her feelings, sympathetic though he might sound. Frank Lorrimer's death was still painful.

"I was actually thinking about the business. It must be a great worry to you to know what to do now. But don't despair, I've come with a plan that will solve all your problems. I'm suggesting that Rutherfords take over the factory — everything, buildings, stock, machinery. Buy you out, in fact. What do you say?"

"What?" Francesca stared at him, open-mouthed. She couldn't believe what she was hearing.

"It makes perfect sense," Howard continued, moving towards her desk. "Rutherfords must be your main customer and if we took over your factory we'd be making our own spares and tools. Much more practical. I realise I should, perhaps, have approached your solicitors first, but I wanted to meet you in person, hence

6

this rather informal approach. I will, of course, have my legal team draw up a proper agreement and contact your solicitors. They're Sutton and Westbury, aren't they?" He mentioned the name of the town's leading firm of solicitors.

"I — I'll have to think about it," Francesca stammered.

"What is there to think about?" Howard seemed genuinely surprised. "We'd be giving you a fair price, better than anything you could expect if you sold on the open market. Come to think of it, *could* you sell this place as a going concern?" He gave a disparaging look round the room. "The business side of the company hasn't been brought up to date, has it? You still appear to be using filing cabinets! And I don't suppose your computer system is less than five years old."

"We haven't exactly — " Francesca began defensively, then stopped. Why should she admit to this man that they barely had a computer system at all?

But he swept on, ignoring her.

"Well, there you are, then! Rutherfords is your best option. Your only option, in fact. We'll make a deal about staff — can't guarantee to keep them all on, of course, but there'll be redundancy payments where necessary, and for yourself, sufficient capital to see you comfortably settled. You'd have spare time and the means to travel, take up some interesting hobbies — a very enviable life of leisure!"

Francesca had the feeling she was being swept along far faster than she wished, and his patronising attitude made her respond unwisely.

"I'm not at all sure that I want to sell the business," she said coldly. "Either to you, or anyone."

"But you can hardly carry on by yourself!" he exclaimed.

"Why not? I worked with my father for years; ever since I left school. The last few years we discussed everything together. I was practically a partner. I'm sure I could continue running

Lorrimers by myself for — well, indefinitely."

"I fear you may find yourself with problems you haven't even thought of yet," Howard replied. "However, I'll leave you to think over what I've suggested. I'm sure you'll see the advantages in it. Talk it over with your financial advisers, perhaps?"

"I'm sure I can already see advantages in the idea from Rutherford's point of view," Francesca snapped irritably. "But I doubt if there is anything to be gained for Lorrimers to be swallowed up by a larger company."

"Better that than face being left behind in business and ending up with a worthless liability," he said smoothly. Then, before she had time to think of an angry retort, he added. "So, when you've thought my proposition over and made up your mind it's the best thing for Lorrimers, I'll expect to hear from you. You know where to find me. Good day to you, Miss Lorrimer." He turned on his heel and strode out of the office. She heard him make some remark to Sally as he passed through Reception in the outer office.

Francesca sat down again at her desk, the letter clutched in her hand now forgotten, as she stared after Howard's retreating figure. Perhaps she should at least have given some consideration to his proposition, she thought. Find out exactly what the details were, though the idea of Lorrimers being absorbed into another, much bigger company and disappearing altogether, was not something she would ever want to happen.

Howard Rutherford had not been the first person to suggest she sold out when her father died. Francesca remembered Mr Sutton giving her fatherly advice as she sat in his stuffy little solicitor's office, two days after her father's funeral.

He had assumed she would want to relinquish responsibility for the factory as soon as possible. Perhaps, she now wondered, he had even suggested to

Howard that the time was appropriate to make her an offer for it.

"It might not be so easy to sell as a going concern, of course," Mr Sutton had said in his ponderous way. "You were doing quite well up to your father's death, but what of the future? We could, of course, try to interest a speculative builder. There's a fair amount of land involved, isn't there? Probably enough to erect a small housing estate. That might be your most lucrative option."

The idea of the factory her father had started up himself, swept away to make room for a housing estate, was a depressing idea.

"I hadn't thought about selling up," she remonstrated faintly. Things were happening too fast. Too much of her world was changing at once.

"But, my dear young lady, what else can you do? Frank had no sons, no one to carry on — "

The slight stung her. "I've worked with my father. He always discussed the business with me. I'm sure I know enough about it — "

"But you don't have any engineering qualifications, I think?" Mr Sutton pointed out.

"No, but I have a good workforce who do. I wasn't planning on working on the factory floor in any case, and I do know about managing the business side."

Mr Sutton shook his head in disapproval. She was young still; she would have to learn the harsh realities of life soon enough, and one of them would be that she'd never manage alone, without her father. Meanwhile, the real purpose of her visit, her father's will, had to be addressed. The main bequest was simple; everything went to her as sole next of kin, but there were one or two details . . .

Francesca let the legal voice drone on, but she wasn't really listening. All this wasn't real; it couldn't be happening. Only a short time ago, less than a week, her father had been alive and well, enthusiastically discussing with her plans for building a staff canteen behind the existing factory shed. "Then the men will be able to have a decent meal at midday, instead of having to bring sandwiches and flasks of tea," Frank had said. "And there'll be a reasonable place to sit and eat, instead of having to park themselves anywhere they can, among the packing cases. They've put up with poor conditions for long enough and it's about time they had some consideration."

They'd mulled over the architect's drawings for a while, then Francesca had cooked supper for them both, as she'd done most nights, ever since her mother's death, ten years previously. They'd watched television for a while, and Frank had worked on a design project for an hour or so, and at eleven o'clock they'd had a last cup of tea together and separated to go to bed.

When Frank hadn't appeared for

breakfast by half past seven the next morning, which was extraordinary for him, Francesca had gone to his bedroom, to find him cold and dead in bed. Died in his sleep from heart failure, the doctor had said.

Overwork, rumoured some, adding that the worry of running a small factory such as Lorrimers must have caused too much stress. Francesca found it hard to believe that could have been the cause. Frank had worries, of course. Who hadn't if they were responsible for the livelihoods of several other people? But Lorrimers was doing well; the business of designing and producing special tools and spare parts for larger engineering companies was something Frank enjoyed and did well. And Francesca, who kept the accounts and looked after the order books, knew there was no cause for worry for the immediate future. Her father had simply had a totally unexpected and fatal heart attack.

The first few days after Frank's death,

Francesca had been so busy dealing with all the hundred and one jobs connected with the funeral, she had had no time to consider the future, either her own or Lorrimers. She was numb with shock, working through the necessary tasks like an automaton, incapable of serious thought. Had it not been for Mavis Roberts, her father's secretary, she might well have forgotten to eat or sleep. Mavis, a widow with a delicate small boy to bring up, had looked after Francesca in those first few days, inviting her home for meals, telephoning to check how she was, if Francesca hadn't been to the office that day, and providing a shoulder to lean on whenever the need arose. The two had always been friends, but Mavis's concern for Francesca over those worst, early days, cemented the friendship into a close bond. Together they sorted out the inevitable problems arising from Frank's untimely death; together they rallied the workforce when no one knew quite what was to happen now, whether or not there would be a future for anyone at Lorrimers. Francesca might have left things to drift on without making any firm decisions, but one Sunday afternoon, some three weeks after the funeral, she looked out of the window of the house she and Frank had shared, the house that had now become depressingly bleak and empty, and saw the day was beautiful without her having noticed; mild and sunny but with the crisp tinge of late autumn. On a sudden whim, she decided to leave all the tasks that had accumulated and take a drive out into the countryside.

She had intended to drive to one of her favourite walking places, a range of low hills some five miles outside Stonebridge, and there do some hard thinking while she strode over the bracken, but she was still so preoccupied with the company's affairs that, without noticing, she automatically took the road she took every morning, and did not realise what she had done until she drove into her

16

parking space in front of Lorrimers factory.

Frank Lorrimer had started his engineering business in the nineteen sixties, buying land and an aircraft hangar from a private flying club which had become bankrupt. The various hangars, some of which dated from the time the land had been a wartime aerodrome, being rented out piecemeal as storage units or workshops to several individuals. Over the years, Frank had bought more land, taking over more buildings as his business had expanded, making specialised tools and spare parts for other, larger companies.

The main machine room was still housed in the original hangar he had first bought, with its enormous double doors, designed to allow access for aeroplanes but now used for the loading and unloading of Lorrimer's fleet of three delivery vans. Over the doors was a faded signboard with the words 'F. Lorrimer; tool engineering and spare parts' written on it.

Francesca got out of her car and stood, looking up at the large building. She rarely saw the place like this, shut and empty with no one else about.

When no one's around, the place almost looks derelict, she thought, looking at the building with new eyes. That sign needs repainting, and it's hanging lop-sidedly. It must have lost a screw from one side. I shall have to remember to tell one of the apprentices to fix it on Monday.

She let herself in by a side door that opened on to the passage between the two offices — Mavis's room which held her desk and typewriter and a row of filing cabinets, and, across the passage, the slightly bigger but still cramped room she had shared with her father. That, too, was lined with filing cabinets. She walked on, through the door which led directly into the machine shop. There was an eerie silence, broken only by the faint hum of the electric generator. Francesca's footsteps echoed up in the roof girders as she paced slowly between the rows of machines.

If I sold out, what would I do with myself, she wondered. Lorrimers had been such a big part of her life, for as long as she could remember. Mr Sutton had hinted, in his rather old-fashioned, pedantic way, that now perhaps it was appropriate for her to consider domestic life, settle down and raise a family, but the idea held no appeal for her right now. She'd had boyfriends, of course, but there had never been anyone she had thought of seriously. At twenty five, she didn't rule out marriage completely, but it was not in her plans for the foreseeable future.

If she didn't sell, would she be able to carry on without Frank? Francesca pondered the idea seriously for the first time as she paced the length of the old hangar. The staff were a good and loyal bunch; almost all of them, apart from the apprentices, had worked for Lorrimers for years. Jim Donovan, the present foreman, had started there as an apprentice, and so had several of the others. They would be relieved if Lorrimers carried on and their jobs were secure, but supposing, after all, it didn't work out and after a few months the orders dried up and Lorrimers was forced to close? Some of the staff, the younger ones and the better skilled, might find other work in the town, but probably not everyone. She had a responsibility for them all.

"Dad, what am I going to do?" She spoke aloud but her voice only echoed back at her in the silence.

Francesca was finding the emptiness of the place depressing, a foretaste of how the building might eventually end. She turned and walked quickly back the way she had come.

What did it matter about the old name board being faded and askew, if she was selling up? Whoever took over would remove it, along with everything else.

She was thinking of all the people she had known, who had worked for her father since Lorrimers had started, and she suddenly remembered Arthur Williams, retired now but still living in the town. He had been her father's first employee, right at the very beginning, before she was born. He had been foreman here for fifteen years, until his retirement, when Jim had taken over.

Getting back into her car, Francesca thought guiltily that she ought to have gone to visit the old man. She had seen him fleetingly at the funeral but there had been little opportunity to speak to everyone individually and she owed it to him, not least for his past loyalty to her father, to call on him as soon as possible. She and Frank had always kept in touch and she knew the house, one in a small terrace of cottages on the far side of Stonebridge, where his unmarried daughter Polly kept house for him. What better time to call in, but now?

"It's very kind of you to call, Miss Lorrimer. Come in, do," Arthur greeted her. "You'll have a cup of tea, won't you?" He ushered her into the little front room, calling out to his daughter "Pol! Miss Lorrimer's here! Make us a brew, will you, lass?"

"A bad business, your Dad going so sudden like that. Shock to us all it was," Arthur continued, settling Francesca beside the blazing fire. "It's good to see you, lass." He beamed with pleasure.

Polly, a buxom, pretty woman in her forties, brought in tea and home made cherry cake on a tray, which she set on a small table between them. Pleased that her father had company, she smiled at Francesca and left them to themselves.

"I was so sorry about your Dad," Arthur said. "Very sudden, too, I heard. Must have been a shock to you."

Francesca nodded. "It's only just beginning to sink in. These last few weeks I've been walking round like a zombie."

"I mind the day I met your Dad," Arthur said reflectively. "Told me he wanted to build a factory that would put the employees first. He knew exactly what he wanted, in his own mind. The old hangar wasn't exactly ideal, by any means, but he was always telling me that one day he'd design a purpose-built place to work in. Would have done, too, in a few more years, I reckon. Just taking a bit longer than he expected."

"I was up there earlier this afternoon," Francesca said. "When it's closed and there's no one around you can really see it for what it is. It's an awfully shabby, run-down looking place now."

"Going to make a few changes, then?" Arthur asked, sipping his tea.

"I don't know. Most people expect that I'll sell out. Mr Sutton assumed I'd be glad to sell the land for a housing estate and live in idleness on the profits."

"But you don't want to do that, do you?"

"No. It would be very sad to see Lorrimers disappear. But if I can't carry on now — "

"Why shouldn't you carry on?" Arthur asked. "You and your father worked together; you must know everything that was in his mind. You've got good men there; that chap as took over from me as foreman — Jim Donovan, wasn't it? — he's a good 'un. And that Mrs Roberts that was your father's secretary, well, I reckon what she don't know about the business side ain't worth knowing. You and she together, now, with the lads you've got there, well, I don't see there's any reason even to think of closing down Lorrimers. With folk like that you could carry on and build up the business just like your father planned to do."

"Do you really think so?" Francesca felt a lightening of her spirits. If Arthur believed in her, then perhaps it was possible to carry on by herself, after all. But he'd been away from the place for some years now, and he was an old man. Did he really know what it would entail? Was he, perhaps, only telling her what she wanted to hear?

"What do you think your father would say? I reckon he'd have been thinking of retiring one day, and when that day came it wouldn't occur to him that you wouldn't be keeping on the place. Didn't make no difference to him that he didn't have a son to take up engineering after him. He used to say to me, Arthur, my daughter's as good as anyone, even though she's not an engineer."

"Did he really say that?" Francesca said doubtfully. Arthur grinned at her. "Well, lass, when you've got plenty of skilled men to work the machines, the really important thing is to get the orders in and the bills paid. And you do that all right, don't you?"

They chatted on for a while, but Francesca had made up her mind. Tomorrow, she would tell them all that Lorrimers was continuing as before, with their help and encouragement, she and they would succeed together. She said goodbye to Arthur and Polly and drove home with a lighter heart than she had felt for weeks.

And then, just as she was dealing with the morning's post that Monday, before going out to speak to the men and tell them her decision, Howard Rutherford had strolled, uninvited, and unannounced, into her office and dropped his bombshell of an offer!

After he'd gone, she sat staring at the doorway, deep in thought. She knew that Mr Sutton, for one, would look upon Rutherford's offer as the best possible solution anyone could have hoped for. She would be urged to agree as speedily as she could and let Rutherfords take over as soon as possible. But she had already made up her mind in another direction . . .

Francesca left her desk and, still clutching the letter she had been reading earlier, stepped across the passage and knocked on Mavis's door.

The older woman was busy typing. She looked up as Francesca entered, then stopped, her hands still poised over the keyboard.

"What's the matter? I heard voices but I didn't know if I should interrupt. I thought it was one of the men."

"No. I've just had a visit from Howard Rutherford, no less." Francesca perched on a corner of the desk. "Sally must have been on her coffee break and there was no one in Reception so he walked straight into my office, unannounced."

Mavis clucked with annoyance. "I'll tell that girl off. She shouldn't leave the desk without telling someone. What kind of security is that? It could have been anyone wandering around the factory."

"Point is, it wasn't just anyone. It was Howard Rutherford and he's made an offer that Rutherfords should take over Lorrimers. Completely."

"Well! And are you going to consider his offer?" Mavis sat back in her chair, regarding Francesca quizzically.

"He came strolling in as if he owned the place already," Francesca said crossly. "He was rude and patronising, and I — I think I was probably rude back."

"I take it you turned his offer down, then?"

"Oh, Mavis, am I being completely mad to even think I can carry on without Dad? You know I'd made up my mind, that I was going to speak to the men at tea break, but now — ! The man made me feel little more than a silly schoolgirl."

Mavis frowned. "I think it would be a shame if you didn't give it a try," she said slowly. "You'd never forgive yourself if you let all this go without a fight. You never know what you can do until you have to try, Fran."

And you'd know all about that, better than most, Francesca thought, regarding her friend. Mavis's life had been a hard struggle to bring up her small son, whose bouts of illness frequently put him in hospital. The evidence of her worries was there in the lines of tiredness round her eyes and the greyness tinging her once pretty brown hair.

"How's Christopher these days?" Francesca changed the subject and the older woman's face lit up briefly.

"He's been a bit better, recently," she said. "I'm hoping he'll start school in the New Year. He's so looking forward to it but I'm a bit worried he won't be able to do as much as the other children."

"I bet he'll be much brighter than most of them," Francesca said. "He can practically read already. He'll be fine; just you see."

"I know he's bright," Mavis said doubtfully. "But he's not very strong and he has asthmatic attacks so frequently. He won't be able to join in with the more boisterous games. And children can be so cruel to someone who is different."

"The teacher will talk to them first; explain why Christopher can't do certain things. They're not all little monsters. I expect there'll be some little girls who'll want to mother him."

Mavis giggled. "I wonder how he'll react to that! There's a month or so yet, and he's got plenty of friends already who understand his problems, so I guess I'm being silly, worrying about him." She turned back to her typewriter. "Mustn't sit around chatting, I've loads to do. Was there anything else you wanted, or did you just come in for reassurance?"

Francesca laughed. "If I did, you've reassured me. I'll speak to everyone at tea break as I arranged. Oh, yes! There was something else!" She remembered the letter, still clutched in her hand, and held it out. "Rather odd letter from Wentworths. They say they didn't receive that consignment of parts they ordered urgently. Know anything about it?"

Mavis took the letter, glancing at it. "I typed the invoice that went in the box with them. I'm sure I gave it to Jim. There's no hold-up with it, as far as I know. I thought the order

had gone out on the twenty fifth."
She consulted a calendar on her desk.
"That's ten days ago. Want me to ask
Jim about it?"

"I'll speak to him myself. Clearly,
whatever happened, the goods have
gone missing and we'll have to send
a replacement order by express. I'll
telephone Wentworths and apologise
and say their parts will be sent at
once."

Francesca took the letter back and
turned to leave. Mavis hesitated, then
said, "What did you make of Howard
Rutherford, then? Apart from the offer,
I mean."

"I suppose he'd have been all
right if he hadn't been behaving
like a complete male chauvinist and
assuming I wouldn't last five minutes
running Lorrimers without Dad. Gave
the impression he thought he was doing
us all a big favour by offering to buy
us out. Clearly, he thought we were a
backward, out-of-date, run down outfit
that no one else would want."

Mavis pursed her lips, looking thoughtful. "Are you sure you don't want to hear the details about his offer, before you announce to everyone that you are planning to carry on?"

Francesca shook her head firmly. "No! I'd made up my mind over the weekend. I did a great deal of thinking and Howard Rutherford certainly needn't think he can switch on the charm and get just whatever he wants because I'm a woman. He's probably used to getting his own way but he'll find I can be just as determined."

"Good for you!" Mavis said. "Pity I missed seeing him," she added innocently. "They say he's quite good looking, as well as being dynamic as a business man."

"Really? Well, I suppose he could be considered that. I barely noticed," Francesca replied, a little too casually. "What else have you heard about him, then?"

"He's known as the best catch in

Stonebridge. Wealthy, good looking, and can be quite charming too, so I'm told."

"Best catch? Doesn't he have a wife? He must be in his thirties." Francesca hadn't meant to show so much interest in the man, but in truth, she *was* curious.

"As far as I know, he's not married. He's supposed to live alone in one of those huge houses up on the hill, overlooking the town. Lovely area. I've never heard mention of a wife, but of course there may be one in the background. He doesn't sound like the kind of person who'd do his own washing up and cleaning." They both giggled at the thought, then Francesca went out to the machine shop to find Jim Donovan.

"I remember Wentworth's order, Miss Lorrimer," the foreman said, frowning as she showed him the letter. "Ted Grant dealt with it and he's usually very reliable. I told him it was urgent. I'll check with him and find out what's happened, and I'll send out replacements straight away and see they're delivered by express. We mustn't upset them. Wentworths are regular customers."

At the morning tea break Francesca gathered the entire staff together, some twenty or so, and told them that, with their help, she hoped to carry on just as her father would have done. There was relief showing on all their faces and a few cheers were raised.

"And I hope to be able to carry out his plans to expand the factory and build a proper canteen and rest room," she added. "It may take a little longer than my father had envisaged, but I'll do it as soon as I can. I want to do all the things he would have done himself had he still been here, and just the way he'd have done them himself. I'm not trained in the way that he was, but most of you are, and if you stand by me and support Lorrimers, I know it can be done."

"I'm delighted to know you've decided

to carry on, Miss Lorrimer," Jim Donovan said, coming up to her afterwards. "Everyone is very relieved about jobs being safe, and we're all a hundred percent behind you."

"Thanks, Jim. I knew I could count on all of you," Francesca replied. Mavis came up beside her. "How's the new baby, Jim?" she asked. A big grin spread over the foreman's face. "He's great," he said proudly. "Six weeks old now. Sometimes he even sleeps all through the night. Susan will be so happy to hear that Lorrimers won't be closing. We've been worried about what might happen, especially now, with the responsibility of a youngster."

"We've all been worrying about the future," Mavis murmured. "Most people have responsibilities and needed to know. Now we'll all have to see that Lorrimers goes from strength to strength. It's all up to us." She and Francesca made to move away towards their offices, but Jim detained Francesca, saying "Miss Lorrimer — about that

Wentworths order. I've made enquiries and it was definitely dealt with the same day, and sent straight to the loading bay. It's certainly very odd that they never received it. However, I've sent off a replacement order and seen to it myself."

"Thanks, Jim. I suppose it's just one of those things. Deliveries do go missing. They may even have lost it their end." With a shrug, Francesca returned to her office.

At home that evening she cooked herself a solitary supper and tried to interest herself in some television, but without much success. The house felt more empty and lonely than it had ever done on the rare occasions when Frank had been away overnight. This place is too big for one, Francesca thought. Perhaps I ought to think about looking for somewhere smaller. A little cottage further out of town, perhaps? I don't think I want to go on living here by myself.

The telephone rang while she was

dozing over a dull play on television.

"Miss Lorrimer? This is Howard Rutherford. I was wondering — would you do me the honour of dining with me tomorrow night? About eight o'clock, shall we say?"

"Now look, Mr Rutherford. I thought I had made it quite clear that I'm not interested in selling Lorrimers, either to you or anyone. If you think — " Francesca began hotly, but he interrupted her smoothly.

"You misunderstand me. I accept entirely that you are not interested in any offers I might make. You made that perfectly clear to me this morning. I meant this as a purely social invitation."

"Oh?" Francesca said, a little gracelessly.

"It occurred to me, as business associates, it was deplorable that we'd never even met before today. I thought I should remedy that. But I repeat, this is a purely social invitation. I won't mention Rutherfords or Lorrimers or take overs or anything like that, unless you bring up the subject yourself."

"You won't?" Francesca said, bemused.

"I promise. The name's Howard, by the way. So you'll accept? And I won't talk business at all."

"That might be rather difficult," she said coolly. "After all, that's all we have in common, isn't it?"

"We don't know that yet, do we? Perhaps I should say this invitation is also in the nature of an apology."

"Apology?"

"I had the feeling I was rather less than polite when we met. It was remiss of me to barge into your office like that without warning and spring a bombshell on you. So if you'll accept my apology — "

"I think I was probably a bit rude myself."

"Then we're quits, Francesca! So you'll come? I thought we should go to the Royal Oak. They do a good meal there." He mentioned the best, and also the most expensive, restaurant in Stonebridge. "So I'll pick you up at your house at eight o'clock tomorrow evening? Don't worry, I know where you live. Till then, goodbye!" The line clicked and went dead. Francesca found herself still holding the receiver.

A dinner invitation! It was hard to take it at its face value. Howard must be hoping to change her mind eventually. The more she thought about it, the more it seemed that acquiring Lorrimers would be an excellent move from Rutherford's point of view. And all the more reason for her to resist being totally absorbed into the bigger company. However, he'd promised this would be nothing more than a social invitation and it would be interesting to see if he kept his word. Smiling to herself, Francesca replaced the telephone receiver. She wondered what her friend Mavis would make of this unexpected turn of events.

2

ON the stroke of eight o'clock Francesca heard a car draw up outside the house, and a moment later, the doorbell rang. She had been ready for the past twenty minutes, growing increasingly nervous as time passed. Don't be ridiculous, she chided herself, you're acting like a schoolgirl on a first date. He's only pretending that it's a social evening; he'll wine and dine you and then make another offer for Lorrimers. That must be what he has in mind. Well, Francesca, you've already made your decision so you'll just have to go on saying no. It will be interesting, though, to see how far he's prepared to go to get my factory; how much he wants to own it.

When she opened the front door Francesca had to admit that Howard looked very attractive in his formal, dark suit, and she was glad she'd taken the afternoon off to look for a new dress and have her hair professionally attended to. Swept up in a sleek chignon, she knew she wasn't going to look out of place, dining at the Royal Oak.

"Come in. I — I'm nearly ready," she stammered. Behind him she glimpsed a silver grey Bentley with a uniformed driver standing beside the door.

Howard stepped into the tiny hall and she was conscious how shabby her home must look. Mavis had told her where he lived and she realised she could probably fit the whole of this house into one of his rooms. What did it matter, she thought defiantly; come to that he could fit the whole of Lorrimers factory into one small corner of Rutherfords Engineering Company. Except she was quite determined that he never would.

"I only need my coat," she said, picking it up from a chair. As they walked down the front path together, Howard remarked, "I normally drive myself. I have a Lotus Elan I'm rather fond of, but tonight I want to enjoy a drink with my meal and I don't approve of mixing the two."

"Very commendable." Francesca wasn't sure what else to say. As he helped her into the back and settled in beside her, he added, "This is actually my father's car. I've borrowed it for the evening and Charters comes with it."

"Your father! I didn't know you had a father! I mean — " Francesca stopped, covered in embarrassment as she realised her remark could be interpreted as having a rather offensive double meaning, but Howard didn't appear to have noticed.

"My father inherited the business from his father, some thirty years ago," he explained. "He's retired now, and has been for about five years, though he still likes to keep an eye on things. He comes to Board meetings and drops into the office occasionally, but I must say, he doesn't interfere with what I do."

"But he's there if you need him." She hadn't meant to say that, not let the wistfulness in her tone show in her words.

"Yes. Believe me, I can understand how you must miss your father. I never met him, but I'd heard nothing but good of him from all quarters."

"The house feels so empty now. I was considering moving to somewhere smaller, a flat in town, perhaps, or a cottage further out. I haven't made up my mind which yet, but certainly I don't want to stay where I am."

"Don't make any changes in a hurry," Howard advised. "That's what everyone says after a bereavement. Take your time."

In spite of her good intentions, Francesca gave an ironic laugh. "That's rich, coming from you! Weren't you trying to hustle me into a big change yesterday?"

Howard looked apologetic. "I suppose,

from your point of view, it must have seemed like that. But I honestly thought you'd be relieved to have the business taken off your hands. I hadn't realised how involved you already were in it."

"I worked with Dad for more than seven years. He treated me just as he would have a son, I suppose. We never talked about the future but I suppose I'd have taken over when he retired. Except that I never thought of him retiring, that was years away."

The car ran smoothly down the main street of Stonebridge, turned a corner and drew up outside the Royal Oak, an old, Tudor style building that boasted a superb restaurant amongst its old world charm.

They were led to a table in a secluded corner, by the head waiter who clearly knew Howard well. The place oozed comfort and luxury; she could well imagine it was expensive to dine here. She'd have to make an effort to be sociable and stop crediting Howard with ulterior motives. Evidently, he meant what he said and talk of any take over would be dropped, at least until he decided she had had enough of running Lorrimers alone. Then, doubtless, he'd try again.

"Tell me," she began, after the waiter had taken their order and departed. "Do you have any interests apart from your business? If we're to avoid talking about our particular companies, it's going to be difficult unless we discover some other subjects."

Howard chuckled, a rich, deep laugh which brought an involuntary answering smile to Francesca's own lips. "I have very little spare time, and I imagine it's much the same for you. I like to relax when I can; eat out, go to a concert or the theatre; play golf on Sundays. That kind of thing."

"I've had very little time for even that," Francesca confessed. "As well as working at Lorrimers I kept house for my father, so evenings and weekends were pretty well filled."

"That's where we men score," Howard said. "We're rarely expected to do our share of the domestic chores. Life's unfair to working women, don't you think?"

Francesca stared at him, unsure whether or not he was making fun of her. "I wouldn't have thought you'd be concerned about unfairness to women," she remarked. "I thought you believed women should keep out of a man's world."

"Because it is unfair to women, that's why," he replied smoothly. "Tell me, am I dining with a militant women's libber, and should I protect myself with some shin guards and a padded jacket? I've seen them in action and, believe me, it's a terrifying sight."

Francesca burst out laughing. "I'm certainly not one of them! I hadn't thought about it, but I suppose I really believe in fairness for people, men and women."

"So do I. So now that we've broken the ice by discovering something we

46

can agree on, tell me what you do in your spare time. You can't work *all* the time. Don't you find time for golf or tennis, or socialising in a club occasionally?"

Francesca shook her head. "No, not really. I spend time with friends, like my father's secretary, Mavis Roberts, and some of the ex staff. But not much else."

"Don't you ever go to any of the local Chamber of Commerce social events? You're a member of that, I assume?"

"No. I know about the Chamber of Commerce, of course, but I've never thought of joining. As I've said, I've had very little time — "

"But you certainly should join! It's a very good way of meeting useful business contacts, as well as their social programme. Almost all the business people of Stonebridge belong, as well as most of the local councillors and other bigwigs. You'd find it very helpful, I can assure you."

"I don't know. I don't really think — " she began.

"They're having a Christmas dinner and dance on the twentieth," Howard continued. "It's the highlight of their year's social calendar. Would you come with me — as my guest? I'm sure you'd enjoy it and you'd meet a great many people. People you'd find useful to know socially, if you're running a business."

It was undeniably true. Frank had mentioned the Chamber of Commerce on several occasions, commenting that he really ought to consider joining; that Lorrimers was probably the only business in Stonebridge that was not represented. Somehow, neither of them had ever got around to applying for membership. Howard's invitation sounded like a good way of finding out more; whether it really would be as useful as he claimed.

"Thank you. I'd like that," she accepted.

"That's settled, then. At the Town

Hall, five days before Christmas! Now, let's have a look at the dessert trolley, shall we?"

The meal was a success, in spite of Francesca's initial misgivings. Howard hardly mentioned Rutherfords or Lorrimers and certainly made no mention of future plans for either of them.

Charters was waiting outside with the Bentley to drive them home. It was not particularly late, but she wondered uneasily if the poor man had managed to have anything to eat himself. He seemed quite resigned to his late night duties, however.

The car drew up outside her gate. Howard got out with her and followed her up the path. With her key in the lock, she turned back to ask, "Would you care to come in for some coffee?"

"Thank you. It's a nice idea but it would be a bit unfair on Charters. He's on duty tomorrow so I ought to let him off as soon as possible."

"Then thank you — " she began,

but he stopped her by taking her in his arms and kissing her gently on her lips. She looked up at him, startled.

"Why, hasn't anyone ever given you a goodnight kiss before?" he asked, amusement in his voice.

"Of course they have!" she retorted indignantly. "It's only I wasn't expecting — "

"Something like this?" He bent his head again and kissed her fully on her mouth. "Goodnight, Francesca. Until the twentieth." He was down the path and out of the gate without looking back. Watching him, she was relieved to see the hedge and a pair of conifer bushes hid them from Charters' view. A moment later and the engine came to life and the car slid away into the darkness.

Mavis was all eagerness next day, to hear how the dinner had gone. "The Royal Oak! That's a lovely place," she said wistfully. "Michael and I went there once for our first wedding anniversary. It's frightfully expensive."

She sighed gently. "I don't suppose I'll ever go there again. Not that I'd want to, it would bring back too many memories." Changing her mood, she continued briskly, "And did he spend the entire evening trying to make you change your mind and sell him Lorrimers?"

"We hardly spoke about work at all," Francesca replied. "He said he accepted that I wasn't selling, and that was that."

Mavis pursed her lips disbelievingly. "He wants Lorrimers! Make no mistake about it!" she said. "He's being very clever about it, that's all."

"I don't think so. He seemed genuinely to want to help me stay in business. Suggested I ought to join the Chamber of Commerce which I might well do. In fact, he's invited me to their Christmas dinner dance at the Town Hall. It sounds a grand affair, so will you come with me at the weekend and help me choose a dress for it?"

"Delighted to. Always enjoy an

excuse to look round the dress shops," Mavis smiled. "And talking about Christmas, how about you spending it with Christopher and me, this year? We'd both love to have you."

"Thanks! I wasn't looking forward to being on my own then," Francesca admitted. "That will be wonderful."

Their conversation was interrupted by Jim, knocking on Mavis's door. One look at his face told them it was bad news.

"One of the vans has broken down," he said, looking grim. "I've had Ted Maitland strip it down but he can't find what the trouble is. I'll have to get the garage to collect it and see what their experts come up with."

"That's a blow! Is there anything else we can use in the meantime?"

"There's the old van that we don't normally use for long journeys," Jim said. "We could do with another van, in any case. Your father was talking about getting one, three months ago." He stopped, looking apologetic.

"Yes, I know. And that means a bank loan. It looks as if that's become an urgent necessity now. I'll make an appointment to see the Bank Manager this afternoon." Francesca made to move back to her own office, but Jim still stood there.

"Was there something else you wanted, Jim?" she asked.

"Well, yes, Miss Lorrimer." He looked uncomfortable. "You remember the order for Wentworths that we had to replace because they didn't receive it?"

"Yes?"

"It's all very peculiar. We've found the original order, crated up in the back of the old van. No one would load anything into that van, we hardly ever use it. All the men in the loading bay know better than that."

"What are you suggesting?"

"Only that it's damned odd. How on earth did Wentworth's order come to be put into the wrong delivery van? I've asked around but no one knows anything about it."

53

"It is odd," Francesca said, frowning. "But at least Wentworths got their replacements safely, so we'll just have to take the originals back into stock. I'll see what I can do about another van this afternoon, Jim."

At lunchtime she told Mavis she would be seeing the Bank Manager that afternoon, and drove into the centre of town. Stonebridge was a compact, attractive little market town, with a few pleasant Georgian buildings in the High Street and several more modern, rather brash looking shops and office blocks tucked away behind them.

Lorrimer's bank was the town's main one; a big, solid looking building with a rather intimidating aspect.

Francesca was asked to wait until the manager was able to see her. She was shown to a comfortable chair beside a low table spread with financial magazines and newspapers. It was outside the manager's office but still in the main banking hall and in full view of the main doors. While she was sitting there, the central revolving doors swung round and Howard strode into the bank.

Oh, bother! Francesca registered in dismay. If Howard saw her, clearly waiting for an appointment with the manager, he'd realise she must be going to ask for a loan, and that therefore Lorrimers wasn't in such a buoyant financial state as she'd led him to believe. Quickly, she picked up a copy of the Financial Times, the largest paper there, and opened it out in front of her. When she warily lowered it, some moments later, Howard was nowhere to be seen.

Five minutes later, Mr Anderson, the Bank Manager, invited her into his office. He was an elderly man with rather old-fashioned ideas about women in business. He had known Frank ever since Lorrimers had started, and because of his friendship with him, listened courteously while Francesca explained their financial position.

"You know, my dear, you'd be far

better off selling the business now that your father — er — that you are left alone," he said. "You say that the order books are healthy, but where are new orders to come from? Once word gets around that Frank Lorrimer is no longer in charge, I fear some of your customers may go elsewhere."

"I don't see why they should," Francesca retorted indignantly. "We have a good team of qualified staff. We're as good as we've always been."

"But will you always have them with you? Your father was a trained engineer. He knew what his staff did and had the knowledge to see they did things correctly," Mr Anderson pointed out mildly. "Whereas you, I think, have no such qualifications?"

"That's true; but my father hadn't worked in the machine shop for years. There was no need, so his qualifications were irrelevant."

Mr Anderson sighed. She was a determined young woman, and clearly wouldn't be warned. "So you want me to advance you enough money to buy a delivery van?" he said. "Surely, you have a contingency fund for replacing worn out equipment?"

"Of course we have! But I didn't expect to have to replace a van so soon. We don't have enough to pay for it," Francesca said.

Mr Anderson leaned back in his chair. "If you are totally averse to selling, then your best move would be to consider going public. Raise money by a share issue. You'd lose some control, of course, but you'd gain financial backing for the schemes your father had in mind. I suggested it to him myself, some while ago."

And he rejected the idea, Francesca thought, remembering. Aloud, she said, "If I were to offer shares someone could buy them all up and take over the company, couldn't they?"

"In theory, yes, that is possible," Mr Anderson conceded. "But in practice hardly likely that one person — "

"It's more than likely! I've had an

offer for Lorrimers already. If I offered shares, he'd have the chance to control my company and I couldn't do anything to stop him. No, I couldn't do that."

"If you've been made an offer for Lorrimers I strongly advise you to consider it." He saw the determination on Francesca's face as she shook her head. He sighed again.

"What do you propose to use as collateral for this loan?" This idealistic young woman must think money was there for the asking.

"Forget a loan, then!" Francesca said in exasperation. "Will you extend our overdraft for another three months? Look at our accounts — if we can only weather this latest setback I'm sure we can repay it and show a profit. Please, Mr Anderson, give me a chance to prove to you what I can do."

She was so like her father. Mr Anderson remembered the eager young man who had come into this office thirty years ago, full of plans and enthusiasm. Anderson himself had been the newly appointed manager and in those days, equally enthusiastic about his work. Something about Frank Lorrimer had appealed to him, and against the advice of more senior bankers, he had loaned a sum which enabled Frank to start his business. He had taken a chance but had been amply vindicated. Now, here was Frank's daughter sitting in front of him . . .

"I'll tell you what I'll do," he said, making up his mind. "I'll extend the overdraft for three months. But I'll also make some enquiries and see if I can find you a backer."

"A backer?" Francesca asked warily.

"Someone who'll be prepared to invest capital in your business. He'll expect interest paid on his money, of course, but it won't be like having a partner. He won't have any control over your running of the business, though if things go wrong he'll undoubtedly ask for his money back."

"A backer, who'd put money in but not want a degree of control? Is this possible?" Francesca asked.

"It might be. I'll see what I can do. There are always people looking to invest. Meanwhile, I'm afraid you'll have to sort your van out by yourself. Or make do with the old one until the backer materialises." He shook hands with her and Francesca found herself outside the office, the interview over. Not very satisfactorily, from her point of view, but she had won an extension of Lorrimer's overdraft, and perhaps things might be better still if this backer Mr Anderson spoke of, materialised.

She was deep in thought, crossing the marble floor of the main banking hall and not looking where she was going. Suddenly, her arm was taken and she was jerked back, out of the path of a flat bed trolley, loaded with sacks of coins, that was being wheeled across the floor.

"You want to watch out," said a familiar voice. "Those things can give you a nasty crack on the ankle, or worse." She looked up and Howard was smiling down at her. Annoyingly, he said, "You look as if you've had a rather uncomfortable session with the manager. Why not come and have a cup of coffee to help you recover?"

She could hardly refuse, though she made the excuse that she needed to get back to work as soon as possible. Howard kept hold of her arm and led her into the Copper Kettle, the inevitable, rather twee teashop in the High Street.

"At least, they do a good cup of both tea and of coffee," he said. "Which would you prefer?"

"Tea, please," she said automatically.

"I'm looking forward to Friday week," he remarked, as the waitress left with their order.

"Friday?" She stared at him blankly.

"The Chamber of Commerce dinner dance! Don't tell me you'd forgotten! How very unflattering!"

"I'm sorry," she blushed. "I wasn't thinking. No, of course I hadn't forgotten."

"The Bank Manager must really have worried you," Howard commented. "You were miles away when you nearly walked into that trolley. Are things really that bad?"

"Bad? No, of course not!" Francesca exclaimed. "I had a lot to think about. Mr Anderson made some positive suggestions. I assure you, far from being bad, things are doing very well at Lorrimers. In fact, I intend to expand soon. I have some major building works planned which I intend to put in hand quite soon." She gulped on the lie. Well, it wasn't exactly a lie. She did intend to start on her father's building plans as soon as practical, but it was doubtful if that would be very soon, and unlikely that Mr Anderson would help her financially with it.

"Good! I'm delighted to hear it!" Howard almost sounded as if he meant it. "You must tell me all about it; what you plan to do, and so on."

Francesca looked at him sharply. Was he mocking her?

62

"You can hardly expect me to divulge Lorrimer's future plans," she said coolly. "You'll have to wait until we're ready to unveil them."

"You're probably right not to say anything at this stage," Howard said. "I'll look forward to hearing and seeing all about it when you're ready."

She wondered uneasily whether he knew it was a bluff. But one day, she vowed, she'd show him.

As soon as she reasonably could, she said goodbye and collected her car from the car park, driving back to Lorrimers.

Mavis shrugged resignedly when she heard the Bank Manager's decision. "I suppose we couldn't expect him to give us a loan for a new van," she said. "He's quite right that it ought to come out of our replacement of equipment fund, and it will do, except that means we don't have funds for it until the end of January. We'll have to make do with the old van until this one is repaired."

"I'll see if Jim has a report on it from the garage," Francesca said.

In his cubby hole of an office off the machine shop, she found Jim on the telephone. He looked up and gestured to her to wait, then quickly brought the conversation to a close.

"That was the garage," he said grimly, replacing the receiver.

"Bad news?" She knew it was before he answered but she hadn't realised quite how bad.

"They've found the trouble. A quantity of sand had been put in the fuel tank," he said.

"Sand? But how could — ?" Francesca stared at him.

"It could only have been put there deliberately. Sand can't get into the tank by itself. It's done quite a bit of damage to the engine — there'll be several parts to replace as well as cleaning out the tank." Jim's face was grey with worry. "What's happening to this place? I thought Wentworth's order was a stupid mistake but now I wonder.

This certainly wasn't a mistake — it was a deliberate attempt to wreck the van. Why?"

Francesca shook her head. "I can't believe anyone would do anything like that on purpose!"

"If not that, then we've someone on the staff who's a complete nutter!" Jim said angrily.

"Any ideas on who could be responsible?"

He shrugged, spreading his fingers wide. "I thought I knew everyone here and would trust them all, completely. Seems I'm not such a good judge of character as I thought."

"It *can't* be anyone here!" Francesca exclaimed. "It must be someone from outside. That's possible, isn't it? Say someone crept in, after work, or a door was left unlocked — "

"I'd have said that was possible with the sand in the tank," Jim said thoughtfully. "But Wentworth's order. Who would know where to hide the stuff? Who but someone from here would know we hardly ever use that van?"

"It's hateful to have to say it, but we'll both have to start watching everyone now," Francesca said. "But why is it happening now? There was never anything like this when Dad was here."

Jim gave her a strange look. "Seems to me," he said, "someone doesn't want Lorrimers to succeed. Either they want to damage the company or they want you to give up running it. Does that give you any clues?"

3

FRANCESCA sat frowning over a column of figures in one of the accounts ledgers. Finally, she got up and went across the passage to Mavis's office. The clack of the typewriter stopped abruptly as Mavis looked up, questioningly.

"I've been thinking. We ought to have a proper computer system for the office," Francesca began. "It's ridiculous in this day and age, to be still using ledgers and filing cabinets. I hate to admit it, but Howard Rutherford was right; this place is still operating in the dark ages."

Mavis looked doubtful. "Aren't computers terribly complicated? I've never worked with anything like that. You can lose entire records if you push the wrong button, can't you?"

"I shouldn't really think so. I was

67

sorting out the office desk drawers a few days ago and came across some leaflets about a system for small businesses like ours. Dad must have been thinking of doing something like that, but he didn't get round to actually ordering anything."

"Everyone seems to have them these days, even corner shops," Mavis said. "I knew your Dad was thinking about it. Perhaps I put him off. I'm scared stiff of anything mechanical."

"And you work right next to machines all day!" Francesca laughed. "There's one scheme that includes a training course. You'd enjoy it; it would make a nice change. You'd learn another skill and, best of all, it's a local firm."

"Sounds good, if we can afford it," Mavis said.

"I wonder if we can afford not to," Francesca retorted. "Perhaps there'll be someone who I can talk to about it tonight. Howard said the Chamber of Commerce was a way of making useful contacts."

"Tonight!" Mavis exclaimed. "Then what are you doing still here, girl? Take yourself off home and spend what's left of the afternoon making yourself glamorous. Or, at least, like a rich and successful businesswoman. You must do justice to that expensive gown we chose last weekend."

"I'm going! I'm going!" Francesca protested. "I only came in here to sound you out about computers."

"Next year's budget," Mavis said firmly. "We have a van to buy first. Now, off with you! Enjoy yourself!"

Francesca had an appointment with her local hairdresser, then she came home and had a long, luxuriant bath. It was still too early to dress so she worked on Lorrimer's accounts again until she realised time was getting on and she would now have to hurry to be ready by the time Howard arrived.

He called promptly with the Bentley and Charters again. It was pleasant being driven through the main streets of Stonebridge now bright with coloured lights and Christmas decorations. There were quite a few people gathered outside the Town Hall to watch the important citizens going inside. Charters opened the car door and, as Howard helped her out there were a dozen flashes from press cameras, clustered round the bottom of the Town Hall steps.

"I'd no idea this was such an important occasion," Francesca murmured in surprise.

"Biggest in the local calendar. Only rivalled by the summer carnival, and only then if the weather's fine," Howard told her as they mounted the Town Hall steps. "The local papers love to have something colourful to print at this time of the year."

They reached the top of the steps, to be greeted in the entrance hall by a reception committee consisting of the Mayor, the President of the Chamber of Commerce, and several other local dignitaries, all accompanied by their wives. It soon became clear that Howard Rutherford was well-known and well-respected among the important citizens of Stonebridge, and Francesca found she was at once being welcomed and accepted as one of themselves, because of him. It was a pleasant sensation, to be treated like an important and valued member of the business community, introduced and spoken to as if Lorrimers was one of the companies which had put Stonebridge on the map, instead of a small, run-down affair operating from an old aircraft hangar two miles out of town.

Howard seemed to be on first name terms with everyone, and Francesca was surprised to discover how many people seemed to know who she was, too, and expressed tactful sympathy over her father's death.

Inside the Town Hall, the main room, used only for the occasional concert and during election times, had been cleared apart from groups of chairs and small tables round the walls. On the raised platform at the far end, a band was playing, just unobtrusively enough to provide a pleasant background to the buzz of conversation.

"Let me introduce you to some people who may be useful to know," Howard said, taking her arm. "Good evening, George," he greeted one man, who rose politely as they approached. Francesca was startled to recognise Mr Anderson, and was amused to register his surprised expression as he saw who Howard's companion was.

"I think you know Miss Lorrimer," Howard added smoothly. He had not missed the Bank Manager's expression and shared Francesca's amusement.

"Turned you down for a loan, did he?" He murmured as they passed on to another group. "Try asking again after Christmas — you might do better."

That might well be true, Francesca thought, and tried not to feel resentful that Howard's name and influence were helping her. What did it matter, if she could negotiate the extra money

Lorrimers needed for so many things? It did matter, she thought uneasily, because she still wasn't sure that with Howard there might not be strings attached to all this helpfulness.

"Let me get you a drink." He stopped a passing waiter with a tray of glasses. "Champagne cocktail, I would think." He smiled at her, handing her a glass. "There's a chap here tonight who might be useful for you to know," he continued, "Philip Renshaw. He owns a computer company; specialises in systems for small businesses such as yours. You should talk to him. I'll try to look him out and introduce you."

It could have been taken as a broad hint that she needed a computer system, which Francesca already knew, but the name distracted her momentarily. It had been the name on the leaflet she'd found in her father's desk drawer in the office, and she'd already decided to pursue the matter further in the New Year. Now, in an informal way, seemed an even better idea.

"Yes, do please arrange for me to meet him," she said meekly.

They were now standing by the main entrance doors to the ballroom, having completed a circular tour round the room, Howard greeting most people by name, and introducing her — "Miss Francesca Lorrimer, owner and Managing Director of Lorrimers Engineering — " to so many of them that she had become bewildered and confused as to who was who; all the names and faces fused into a blur so that now she could not remember anyone.

The President of the Chamber of Commerce and his wife came into the room behind them, having greeted the last of the evening's guests in the entrance hall. He spoke warmly to Howard and it was clear they were good friends. Meanwhile, his wife smiled in a friendly way at Francesca. After a moment, Howard turn to her and said, "Francesca, there's a chap across the room I wanted a word with. Purely business, so do you mind if I leave you with Sir John and Lady Rivers for a few moments?"

"Of course not," she replied.

Howard walked across the floor and the President's wife said, "Why don't we sit down, my dear? There's a table reserved for us somewhere round here."

Sir John led the way, and the moment they were seated, two waiters arrived with a selection of drinks and a dish of canapés. Francesca was beginning to enjoy herself. Not only was she among all the influential citizens of Stonebridge, but she was sitting with the most important of them, being treated as if she, too, was a businesswoman of standing. "And Lorrimers will be up there, amongst the important companies, one day," she vowed, taking a sip of her second Champagne cocktail.

" — so sorry to hear about your father, Miss Lorrimer. It was a sad blow to all the town." Sir John had been speaking to her and she dragged her attention back to him.

"We can ill afford to lose men like Frank Lorrimer. There aren't many like him these days, a man who can build a successful small business up from nothing, single-handed."

"Thank you," Francesca murmured. She didn't know what else to say.

Lady Rivers leant across to press her arm encouragingly. "He was very proud of *you*. I knew your father slightly, we were on the committee of a local project last year and his pride in the way you worked with him was very evident."

"You're very kind." Francesca wished they'd change the subject. Frank's death was too sensitive an issue still, to be talked about in a place like this. It would be appalling if she were to shed tears here.

"I'd just like to say, Miss Lorrimer, that I think you're doing the right thing now," Sir John added, sounding slightly pompous.

"You do? Thank you," Francesca

said vaguely. The Champagne cocktail was making her feel slightly muzzy and she hoped it wouldn't be too long before they sat down to dinner. She needed more than a canapé or two to counteract the effects of the alcohol.

"Yes, indeed. Things have changed vastly since your father started Lorrimers. Even he would think twice before embarking on such an enterprise these days."

"Oh, really?" Francesca wasn't following his conversation, but hoped that a few polite monosyllables would be enough until Howard returned to rescue her.

"Yes. Running a small business is so much more complicated today. But you've very sensibly avoided all those future problems. Handing over to Rutherfords must undoubtedly be a great relief to you. You're lucky that they made you an offer so promptly — "

"What?" Francesca suddenly woke up to what Sir John was saying. "No, you've got it all wrong," she said indignantly, "I don't know where you heard that story, but I assure you it's completely untrue. Rutherfords is *not* taking over Lorrimers. Not now; not ever."

Sir John looked startled by her vehemence. "Oh, dear! Miss Lorrimer, I'm so sorry if I've spoken indiscreetly. I had no idea it was still a confidential matter. It just seemed so much the logical answer, with Rutherfords being a similar, local company — "

"It's not confidential! I'd be glad if the whole town knew that I am not interested in selling out to anyone!" Francesca was not aware that she had spoken loudly, but several heads turned at nearby tables.

"I seem to have dropped a brick," Sir John said, looking embarrassed. "I am most sincerely sorry, but you must admit it was a natural assumption, with Lorrimers being so much your father's own, and then seeing you here tonight with Howard Rutherford."

"I worked with my father for years. Many of our decisions were joint ones. I'm confident I can continue in the way he would have done," Francesca said, dropping her voice but sounding very determined. Sir John pursed his lips, looking doubtful. "I hope you know what you are taking on, young lady," he said. "Your father was a qualified engineer. Are you?"

Francesca flushed. "No. But I have some very able and highly-trained men on the staff," she said coldly.

"Not quite the same thing. If Rutherfords should make you an offer in the future, my advice to you would be to consider it very carefully. The alternative might prove a disaster for both you and your staff."

Francesca was close to losing her temper. "I came here tonight as Howard's guest, because he thought it might be helpful to me to join the Chamber of Commerce and meet other business people. If all I am going to get is advice to sell out my company because people don't think I am capable of running it alone, then perhaps joining isn't going to be such a good idea after all."

"I'm sorry you feel like that," Sir John said courteously. "I hope you will join the Chamber, and I apologise if I have offered unwelcome advice. It's what I would have said to your father if Rutherfords had made an offer to him."

Francesca felt ashamed and embarrassed by her outburst. She didn't know what to say. Why did the suggestion of her selling out to Rutherfords always touch a raw spot with her?

"Never mind, my dear. You go ahead and show us all what women can do these days," Lady Rivers whispered to her, patting her arm again.

Howard returned to their table at that moment, saving her further embarrassment. "I'm sure you'd like to dance," he said, and, although her dancing was very rusty and she was nervous about partnering him with her limited skills, she stood up with relief at being offered an escape.

She didn't mention her conversation with Sir John to Howard. She was too busy concentrating on dancing, although Howard was a very good dancer and made her feel her own lack of expertise didn't matter.

Afterwards, he took her to meet Philip Renshaw, who was helpful and knowledgeable about computer systems for companies such as Lorrimers, and seemed to know exactly the kind of package she needed. He promised to be in touch with her in the New Year and told her of a rental deal for the system which would make it possible to install without a vast initial outlay. Francesca's spirits began to lift and she forgot about the conversation with Sir John and his wife.

Shortly afterwards they went in to dinner, to a splendid meal laid out on long tables in one of the large council chambers. Howard was seated opposite her, and her two immediate neighbours were strangers. On her right, a middle-aged man with a paunch, introduced himself as the owner of a chain of grocery stores with branches within a fifty mile radius of Stonebridge. He'd never heard of Lorrimers, and since her company had little to do with food in any way, he soon lost interest and transferred his attention to his neighbour on his other side.

The neighbour on her left was elderly, a retired businessman who seemed surprised that Francesca actually ran a business of any sort. He clearly disapproved of women in the workplace in anything but a very minor role. "Tea and typing," he said ponderously, was the rightful place for women until they left work for marriage, their natural occupation. Francesca was beginning to become rather annoyed by his attitude, and her discomfiture was not helped by Howard, who, hearing snatches of the man's monologue, grinned and winked at her, nodding his head in mocking agreement.

"Of course you'll sell out. No woman could possibly handle an engineering business. That's men's work," the man announced. "Put everything into the hands of your company solicitor. Don't try to do anything yourself; sure to be a disaster. Then, when you have the money, you'll be able to look for a nice husband and settle down. Raising a big family will keep you fully occupied. Keep you out of mischief, at any rate."

Francesca's face flamed with fury. She dared not reply in case she was very, very rude and embarrassed everyone. She was already conscious that her earlier outburst in front of the President and his wife had been noticed by several people nearby. They probably wouldn't ask her to join if she kept losing her temper with members, and Howard would certainly be embarrassed by her behaviour. She looked across at him. He was clearly amused by the man's opinions and her reaction to them. Deliberately, he leant across and spoke to the man. "Excellent idea, keeping women out of business. Save us no end of trouble, eh? Keep 'em all tied to the kitchen sink."

The man looked up, warily. He was sharp enough to wonder whether he was being made fun of, but Howard's expression was bland.

"Glad to see some commonsense in the younger generation," he mumbled.

"I've been trying to save Miss Lorrimer from her life of drudgery and business worries, but she seems to prefer that to a life of idle luxury." Howard leered at Francesca as he spoke, and she wished she could kick him under the table, but the chairs were close together and she didn't dare risk her aim.

The food was excellent, but Francesca barely noticed what she ate. She longed for the meal to be over so that she could escape from her dinner companions.

At last, the coffee cups were emptied, the last liqueurs drained, and people began leaving the table. "If you'll excuse me, I'll find the ladies' room," she said briefly to Howard, walking away and leaving him still at the table. She found her way to the ladies' powder room, full of women gossiping amongst themselves. To her relief, no one gave her a second glance, although she dawdled at the mirrors, fiddling with her hair and lipstick unwilling to go out and face Howard.

She had to leave eventually; there were others wishing to use the mirrors. When she returned to the main hall, Howard was nowhere to be seen. Francesca stood watching the crowd. A few had returned to the dance floor, but most were standing in groups talking like the old friends they undoubtedly were. It struck her then, how few people she really knew, considering she had spent all her life in Stonebridge. She hadn't kept up with schoolfriends, telling herself she was too busy; that working beside her father took up all her time and, anyway, was all she needed. Now, she wished she had more friends people who could advise her impartially. There was Mavis, of course, as loyal a friend as one could possibly want, but Mavis's advice on Lorrimers was bound to be influenced by her own views, her own desperate need to keep her job for Christopher's sake. Tonight had been intended as her first opportunity to meet other business people in Stonebridge, but it had all gone horribly wrong.

"Are you by yourself or are you just about to join one of these exclusive groups?" Someone spoke at her elbow. She looked up quickly, into a pair of blue eyes in an open, smiling face. Their owner was slightly taller than herself and looked about the same age. She was instinctively drawn to him.

"Well, I appear to be by myself at the moment," she said. "And it's unlikely I'll be joining any of those groups. I hardly know anyone here."

"Ah! I was right, then! You looked a little lost, just like I feel," he said. "It's my first experience of

Stonebridge social life and I'm finding it a bit overwhelming. My name's Geoff Baxter, by the way, and I'm a pharmacist. I've been in Stonebridge just a week."

"I'm Francesca Lorrimer. I've been in Stonebridge all my life and I still don't know who most of these people are," she said.

"What hope is there for me, then?" He smiled at her. "Well, we've met each other and that's a start. Would you care for a dance?"

He danced well, though not with the panache that Howard had displayed. Francesca found him easy to talk to. He told her he had come to Stonebridge to work in the chemist's shop in the High Street. He had come from the London suburbs where he'd had a small shop. His wife had died, tragically young, just six months ago and he had come north, to Stonebridge, to try to put all the past unhappiness behind him.

"But that's enough about me," he said, having briefly sketched in his

87

background. "What about you? What work do you do in the town?"

Francesca told him about Lorrimers and he sympathised over her father's death. "But the only way is to forge ahead. Don't dwell on the past," he said. "Put all your energies into building up your company. You've a good base; build on it."

"I'm having doubts — " Francesca began. "So many people seem to think that a woman can't, or shouldn't, run a business in such a male dominated industry."

"Don't have doubts! Take no notice of what anyone says. You always encounter the doom merchants who enjoy seeing people fail. Makes their own efforts seem less feeble. Go for it, Francesca! I can see you're the sort of girl with the guts to succeed. I'd put my money on you, any day."

With that kind of encouraging speech, Francesca's spirits rose considerably. She had two more dances with Geoff, almost forgetting Howard, and then the secretary of the Chamber of Commerce bore down on them while they were pausing between dances, and asked if he might take Geoff to meet the President. "Sir John apologises that he hasn't been able to welcome you properly tonight," the secretary said, flustered. "Matter of fact, I was looking for you earlier to bring you to him, but I couldn't find you. If you wouldn't mind interrupting your dance for a short while, I'll take you to Sir John's table."

"Summoned to the presence!" Geoff said, smiling at Francesca. "I hope I may see you again soon. You know where to find me in working hours." He went off with the Chamber of Commerce secretary and Francesca was left by herself.

Not for long, however. "Oh, *there* you are!" Howard was beside her. "I was looking for you. I wondered if you wanted to dance, but it seemed you were not in need of a partner."

Francesca was still annoyed with him

over the jibes at the dinner table. "I met someone who doesn't seem to think a woman's place is in the kitchen," she said coldly. "Very refreshing."

"It's hardly my fault if people come to the obvious conclusion, that a larger engineering company will take over a smaller one," Howard said. "They thought that themselves; I didn't say anything."

Francesca didn't want to be drawn into further argument. She suddenly felt tired, weary of continually having to justify her position at Lorrimers.

"Howard — if you don't mind I think I'd like to go home now," she said. "I'm not used to late nights."

"Of course, if you wish. I'll get Charters to bring the car round and I'll get my coat."

"You don't have to come, if you want to stay on," she said quickly. "Charters can take me and come back for you later, if you prefer."

"But of course I'll escort you home!" He looked askance. "Fetch your coat and I'll find Charters."

When Francesca came out into the entrance hall she nearly bumped into an elderly man who was having a quiet smoke by the door.

"Why, good evening, Miss Lorrimer! Fancy seeing you here!" he exclaimed.

"Hello, Fred!" She smiled at the man who had been her local butcher for years. He owned three shops now, in different parts of Stonebridge, but she remembered him behind the counter when she had been a child, dropping in on her way home from school to buy something for her father and herself for their evening meal.

"Quite the businesswoman yourself now," he said. "Nice to see some youngsters here. It's mostly old fogies like me who come to these do's. That's why they have those old-fashioned dances and such. I was sorry to hear of your father's passing, Miss Lorrimer. He'll be sorely missed, I reckon."

"Thank you," Francesca said automatically. She glanced round. There was no sign of Howard or Charters with the Bentley.

"I expect you'll be selling up the business now, won't you?" Fred continued. "No one to carry on, like."

"Not at all!" Francesca said sharply. "I'm carrying on."

He looked at her in disbelief. "You sure that's wise, Miss Lorrimer? For a couple of months maybe, but surely not longer. I heard as how you were selling out to Rutherfords — "

"Who told you that?" she demanded.

"Young chap I was speaking to. Well, I suppose it's all a bit premature so I won't say any more. Read about it all in the papers, no doubt." Before she could answer, he stubbed out his cigarette and moved towards the main hall. "Goodnight, Miss Lorrimer!" he called over his shoulder.

Francesca watched him go, speechless with indignation. She moved out of the main doors on to the steps to look for Charters and the car. Suddenly, she wanted to be away from this place as soon as possible.

A young man with a notebook in his hand and a camera slung over one shoulder, came up the steps towards her.

"Miss Lorrimer?" he asked.

"Who are you?" she asked, warily.

"Kevin Thompson, reporter on the Stonebridge Gazette. I wrote the obit. for your father last month."

"Oh, yes, I remember!" He'd come to see her at the factory, had been pleasant and sympathetic and written a surprisingly accurate report about the history of Lorrimers.

"Your father was an exceptional man, Miss Lorrimer. The more I researched for the article, the more I regretted that I had never met him in person."

"Thank you," Francesca said mechanically. It was nice to know her father had been so well respected in the community. She wondered if Frank had ever realised this before he died. She glanced along the road. No sign of Charters yet.

"I was sorry to hear the latest news about Lorrimers," Kevin continued. "Though I suppose it was inevitable."

"Quite." She hadn't been listening, wishing he'd go away. Everyone spoke of Frank; they didn't to expect Lorrimers to have a future, only a past.

"So how do you feel about it, Miss Lorrimer?"

Francesca dragged her mind back to the reporter. "Feel about what?" she asked vaguely.

"About Lorrimers."

"Oh, very confident," she replied. "I'm sure in the future Lorrimers will go from strength to strength."

Kevin looked puzzled. "You are obviously very pleased about the tie-up with Rutherfords, then?"

"What?" It suddenly dawned on her what he had been saying. She turned on him, annoyed with herself for not paying more attention, anxious about what wrong impression she might have given.

"Please understand. There is no tie-up with Rutherfords. My company is not selling out, or doing deals with anyone. Lorrimers will continue as before — "

Howard came out of the main door and ran lightly down the steps, just as the Bentley, with Charters at the wheel, swept up beside them.

Howard flung open the rear door. At the same moment Francesca was aware that the young reporter had his camera ready, and several flashes told her he was using it on them both.

"Oh, no!" she gasped, as Howard settled himself beside her and Charters pulled away from the kerb.

"What's wrong?" Howard asked.

"That reporter — he's another one. He was asking me — he assumed, like everyone else tonight, that Rutherfords was taking over Lorrimers. Now, he'll be sure it's true, in spite of anything I've said."

"You must admit it's what many people will naturally assume," Howard said easily. "Why let it worry you? In a few months, when they see it hasn't happened, people will forget they ever thought it might. Don't get so uptight about it."

"You're enjoying the situation!" Francesca said crossly. "Everyone assumed I would be only too relieved to sell out to you and I can only think that was because someone had led them to believe that was the case. And your behaviour at the dinner table was outrageous," she continued. "If you say things like that to people — "

"Utterly unforgiveable," Howard agreed. "But you surely didn't think I really meant it."

"That awful man did."

"Why bother with him? His views were out of the dark ages anyway. Nothing I could have said would have changed his opinions."

"I believe you were so sure I'd accept your offer for Lorrimers that

96

you told the President and lots of other people even before you spoke to me!" Francesca said wildly.

"I don't make a practice of discussing my business plans with people who have nothing to do with Rutherfords," Howard said stiffly. "But as to my offer; it's a good and fair one. It's still open. You might still change your mind and decide to see what I'm offering."

"Never!" Francesca said vehemently.

Howard sighed. "Never is a long time," he said quietly. "Situations can change. Well, we'll see. The offer is still there for a while yet."

Francesca seethed silently beside him. She was convinced now that that whole evening had been planned so that certain people, important, influential people whose advice she might have been expected to heed, would show her that selling out to Rutherfords was the best way forward. They must have been laughing at me, she thought bitterly, an inexperienced girl in her twenties, thinking she could manage to run an engineering business by herself. They must have thought I was completely insane. But I'll show them, she thought, though with somewhat less conviction than she had felt earlier.

Howard said nothing more and they sat in silence until Charters drew up outside her house. He didn't make any move to get out of the car with her, but Charters accompanied her up the path to her front door.

"Would you like me to step inside, Miss? See it's all as it should be? It's not too pleasant coming into an empty house, late at night," he offered.

"That's kind of you, Charters, but I really don't think it's necessary." Francesca was touched by the man's thoughtfulness, but she longed to be on her own, wanted nothing more than to see Howard and his Bentley disappear into the night and leave her to herself.

She went inside and closed the door. Moments later, she heard the car drive away. Wearily, she walked slowly upstairs. The night, which had begun so well, had ended disastrously. She'd quarrelled with Howard and after tonight she doubted if she'd ever see or hear from him again. Except, of course, when he was in touch to see if she'd changed her mind about selling.

Although it was late and she was tired, Francesca lay awake for a long time. She was disappointed, sorry that circumstances had wrecked the friendship that had been developing between them. If he wasn't who he was, an opportunist who was after her factory, she might have liked him very much indeed.

She was, for once, late into work the following Monday. To her surprise, Mavis's desk was empty, the cover still over her typewriter and the mail still lying on top of a filing cabinet inside the door, where one of the apprentices had left it. She picked up the pile of letters and began to sort them.

Half past ten, Mavis came hurrying into her office, still in her coat. "Fran,

I'm sorry! Christopher was taken ill in the night and I've been at the hospital. I tried to phone you but all the call boxes were out of order. Whatever must you have though of me?"

"I was worried; you're so rarely absent," Francesca said. "But you shouldn't be here now! Go back to Christopher. I can manage here."

"No. He was asleep when I left and I'm better working. There's plenty to do." Mavis seized the pile of letters Francesca had sorted and turned to go out to her own office.

"What happened?" Francesca asked.

"The usual trouble! He was quite frighteningly bad last night, but once he was in hospital and they'd given him some medication and an inhaler, he was much better. They're keeping him in for a few days, the doctor said. Little monkey, he'll be in over Christmas. He's pleased as Punch about that; they always give the children a wonderful time, far better than he'd get at home. He was in the last two Christmases; I told him I was sure he'd had an attack on purpose."

The worry in Mavis's clear grey eyes belied her words. Francesca looked at her friend anxiously. "Shouldn't you at least be at home, in case the hospital telephones?" she asked.

"I gave them this number. No, Fran, I'd rather be here, with people, than alone at home," Mavis insisted. "I wouldn't visit again until this evening, anyway. No point in sitting there while he's sleeping."

"You down tools and go off to the hospital whenever you want," Francesca ordered.

"It's still on, I hope, for you to come to me for Christmas Day?" Mavis paused by the door. "We can go and visit in the afternoon. I'd be even more glad of your company for lunch now."

Jim Donovan appeared in the doorway leading from the machine shop. "Bad news from the garage, I'm afraid," he said. "There's a delay in getting replacement parts for the van. Pity we can't make them ourselves. Is it possible to get hold of another van temporarily, do you think? We'll be desperately hard pressed by the end of the holiday."

"You could borrow one!" Mavis exclaimed. "Ask Howard Rutherford! You must be really good friends by now, especially after Friday's dinner dance. I completely forgot to ask you how it went. He'd surely let you have one for a few weeks; Rutherfords has a whole fleet of the things."

"I don't really think — " Francesca began.

"That would be a convenient solution, Miss Lorrimer," Jim said. "Perhaps you could ask? I don't see what else we can do. It's not easy to hire vans of that size. It would be only for a couple of weeks, but we'll certainly have a problem in January if we haven't found something by then."

"I — I'll see what I can do,"

Francesca said faintly. Borrow a van from Rutherfords! That was the last thing she wanted, to beg a favour from Howard, show him that already Lorrimers needed his help.

4

THERE was something more worrying waiting for her when Francesca arrived home that evening. The local paper had been delivered and was lying on the mat. As she opened it out, her face drained of colour. Among the captions to the series of pictures taken at the Chamber of Commerce dinner dance, one headline sprang out at her: 'Rutherford's Bid for Lorrimers.' Underneath, a subtitle added 'Lorrimers happy with arrangement, but is a takeover all that's involved?' Below that was a picture of herself and Howard getting into the Bentley. The whole article that accompanied the picture was speculation and innuendo — suggestions that there might be more behind the proposed take over than a mere business transaction — that there might be some personal and romantic link between the people involved. The article was a clever one; Francesca had to admit that. No outright facts that were indubitably untrue, just implications and the comment that in answer to questions about the rumour regarding Rutherford's take-over, Francesca Lorrimer, 'heiress to Lorrimer's Empire' told the reporter she was 'happy with the arrangements that had been made.' The picture of herself and Howard implied more than the reporter would have dared print.

"This is awful!" Francesca gasped. "Did I really say that? What, exactly, did I say?"

Her first instinct was to telephone Howard. He should be as embarrassed and annoyed as she was, by the whole thing. Then she hesitated; it would be embarrassing to speak to him after the way they had parted after the dance. He might be as furious as she was but it seemed far more likely he would be amused. As far as he was concerned, the more people who thought Lorrimers was being taken over by his company, the better. In time it might become true.

What was her staff going to think, she worried. She decided to telephone the Gazette's editorial office first thing in the morning and ask them to print a correction. It was difficult, because what they'd printed was, in effect, no more than what she'd said to Kevin Thompson. It had been quoted out of context and a quite different slant put upon it.

Francesca spent a restless night. She arrived at the factory early, but Mavis was there already, busy typing in her room.

"How is Christopher?" Francesca put her head round the door.

"Quite cheerful. They're keeping him in until after Christmas — perhaps that's why he's cheerful," Mavis said ruefully. "I came in early to clear up as much as I could — would it be all right if I went early this evening? I'd like to be at the hospital by four."

"Of course. I told you to take off as much time as you needed." Francesca made to move off towards her own office but Mavis gestured with one hand towards a folded newspaper on the top of her letter tray.

"Did you see yesterday's local?"

"I did. You know none of it's true, don't you?"

"I do. At least, I hoped it was all some horrible mistake. But I've heard a few remarks out in the machine shop — you'd better talk to them and reassure them. Some of the married men are worried about the uncertainty."

Francesca spoke to the assembled staff at teabreak that morning. She reassured them that the local paper had assumed far too much, and the fact that Howard Rutherford had invited her to the Chamber of Commerce dinner dance did not indicate any closer links, either with his company or personally. "In fact, I hope I squashed several inaccurate rumours about Lorrimer's future, that evening," she concluded. "We're carrying on. Next year we'll be doing even better."

"I hope you're on good enough terms with Mr Rutherford to speak to him about a van," Jim said to her afterwards. "We'll need something straight after the Christmas break. It's that that's causing the delay with repairs to our damaged one. Everything stops at that garage for nearly ten days, so they've told me."

"I'll see what I can do," Francesca replied. It would be no good telephoning Rutherfords and speaking to a member of staff. No one but Howard would be able to authorise such a loan, but he'd be likely to make her eat humble pie before he agreed, if he agreed at all. Leaving Lorrimers with delivery problems would no doubt suit his plans very well.

The Christmas break came as a relief; an excuse to stop worrying about Rutherfords, even if only for a day. On Christmas morning she drove over to Mavis's home and together they cooked a Christmas meal. The hospital discouraged visitors before the afternoon and so they planned to visit Christopher after listening to the Queen's speech.

"I'm making a New Year resolution," Francesca confided as they climbed into the car to drive to the hospital. "I'm going to change my life. As soon as the estate agents open again in the New Year I'm going to start looking for a new home, something smaller, more manageable. A country cottage, I think. Not too far out but more on the outskirts of Stonebridge. My house is far too big for me alone and it's too full of the past. I want to make a new beginning."

"I know how you feel," Mavis sympathised. "When Michael died, I thought of moving. But it's different with a husband. We'd chosen the house together and it was so full of him, full of memories. In the end, we stayed put. Plenty of room for Christopher as he grows up. But in your case, I'd definitely think of finding a little place of your own."

They walked into the children's ward to find Christopher propped up in bed, looking well and excited. "Look, Mum!" he greeted Mavis, "Father Christmas came last night and left me this game. And, you know what? Nurse says he's coming back *again* today when he's finished visiting all the other children in their homes!"

"You certainly look very well," Francesca said, dropping her own gift on to the bed for him. He pulled away the paper eagerly and held up the toy in delight. "Gosh, a fire engine! Thanks, Auntie Fran! That's smashing!"

They stayed in the ward for about an hour, talking to Christopher and some of the other patients and their parents, then, at half past four, they sensed a ripple of excitement amongst the young patients. "They know what's going to happen," said the Sister in charge, pausing beside Christopher's bed. "Just like last year, isn't it, Christopher?

Hark, you can hear the sleighbells if you're very quiet."

"Does he really leave his reindeers in the car park?" Christopher asked curiously.

Then they all heard the jingle of handbells in the passage outside. The doors were pushed open and in strode a character who was every inch the Father Christmas of every child's dreams. Even Francesca felt herself swept up into the fantasy as she watched the rotund, larger-than-life figure in red tunic, cloak and knee boots stride down the ward between the rows of beds. His hood was up, but masses of white, curly hair showed beneath it, and the lower half of his face was obscured by a long, bushy cotton wool beard that reached half way down his chest. The beard, though, could not hide his beaming smile as he called out "Happy Christmas, children!" and his eyes twinkled as he lowered an enormous sack from his shoulders on to the floor.

Squeals and gasps of excitement greeted his arrival, but this was no ordinary, dressed-up impersonator. Francesca, watching from Christopher's bed, could see at once that he was the ideal of a Santa Claus. He stopped by each bed in turn, talking to the child in it with no false jollity but a friendliness and genuine interest. And he seemed to know every child's name.

"It's amazing!" Mavis whispered. "He's absolutely wonderful with all of them! He must be one of their best pediatric doctors, I should think."

"How else would he know their names?" Francesca replied. "He reminds me of my own childhood. He's straight out of 'The Night Before Christmas.'"

"Is he really like that, or is it clever padding?" Mavis wondered. "He must be a huge man if it's real. I thought I knew most of the doctors here by now, but I don't remember seeing anyone as large as him. Perhaps he's one of the visiting consultants!"

After he had handed out presents to

each child in turn, Father Christmas returned to his largely depleted sack by the ward Christmas tree and plunged his hands into it again.

"What have we here?" he boomed. "A present for Sister, no less!" He held up a gaily wrapped packet, waving it around as he looked up and down the ward for Sister's dark blue uniform. Pretending surprise and shyness, she was persuaded forward by shouts from the children, and accepted her present and a whiskery kiss from Santa He went through the entire staff; each nurse, ward orderly and even the cleaners, was called up by name and given a small present from Santa's sack.

"Isn't he splendid?" Sister Woodrow had paused by Christopher's bed to show them all the bottle of perfume she had received. "This is lovely stuff. If only I dared wear it on duty! Do you know, he comes to the children's ward every year, and never misses anyone out? It's enough to make anyone believe in Santa Claus, even an old cynic like me!"

"Who is he? One of the doctors?" Mavis asked.

"The odd thing is, nobody actually seems to know. I'm pretty sure he's not on the staff, but he must have a good intelligence system; he knows what children we have in, how many girls and boys and what ages they are. The presents are always very appropriate. My guess is that he's a local businessman or, more likely, someone on the staff of one of the big shops, sent by the management. He certainly has a way with the children."

Francesca was watching Christopher, his eyes shining, hugging a big, golden teddy bear and at the same time thumbing through a colouring book, complete with a pack of crayons. He looked dazed and kept turning to stare at the red suited man by the Christmas tree.

"It really is true, Mum! There really

is a Father Christmas after all," he whispered. "And I thought it was you all the time!"

Francesca glanced at Mavis and saw she was fighting back tears. She leaned over the end of the bed and gave her friend a quick hug. "Both Chris and I are having the best Christmas ever!" she said, and meant it.

At the far end of the ward, Father Christmas had upended his sack to show the children there were no more presents. He was making jokes and the children giggled until they were weak with laughter.

"There's just one more thing before I go." Father Christmas held up his hand to gain their attention. "This morning, when I called at one of the houses in the town to deliver a present, I couldn't get down the chimney." There were hoots of laughter at the idea of this rotund character getting down any chimney. "So I brought the present with me, in case by any chance the person happened to be here. I'm glad to see she is, so if she'll come up and kiss me under the mistletoe, she can have it." He held up a small parcel, no more than two inches square. "Of course, I could have dropped it through the letterbox, but where's the fun in that?" He gave a loud, false guffaw. "I'd have missed out on a kiss, wouldn't I?" While everyone waited to see what would happen next, he called out, "So would Francesca Lorrimer please come up and receive her present from Father Christmas?"

Francesca gasped. Why her, when there were at least two visitors to every bed in the ward? Clearly, it was some kind of Father Christmassy joke and she'd be a spoilsport not to go along with it. Slowly she got up from Christopher's bed and walked the length of the ward towards the red tuniced figure. He stood there, in front of her, the present dangling just out of reach, and one arm raised above his head, holding a sprig of mistletoe which he had somehow produced from somewhere.

She was within a foot of him and all she could see were the twinkling brown eyes between the bushy beard and the mop of fake white curls. But the eyes were mocking her, and they looked familiar —

"You!" she gasped. "I've never have believed for a moment — "

"Shh! Don't give me away! I've been doing this for four years and no one's rumbled me yet," Howard hissed back at her. "Play along please, Fran."

She decided to get her own back. "Ooh, thank you, Santa!" she giggled. "I'll give you a kiss but I'm a bit big to sit on your knee." She made a grab for the present but he jerked it out of reach. "Kiss first," he demanded.

Francesca leaned forward and gave him a polite peck on his whiskery cheek. He enveloped her with both arms, kissing her soundly but rather awkwardly through the mass of beard. "That will have to do for now," he whispered. "Take your present. I'll telephone you tomorrow."

"I didn't know Father Christmas brought presents for grown-ups, too," Christopher said innocently, as she returned to his bedside.

"What's the matter, Fran? You've gone quite white as if you'd seen a ghost," Mavis said, looking at her friend.

"It's nothing. I was a bit surprised, that's all," Francesca replied. She thrust the package into her pocket and turned to join in with everyone waving and calling out their goodbyes as Father Christmas left the ward, striding down between the beds and through the swing doors at the end. Faintly, down the passage, they heard again the jingle of bells.

"Do you think he *really* drives his sleigh down the corridor?" Christopher asked, his eyes big as saucers. His bed was littered with discarded wrapping paper and his new acquisitions covered the table over the bed. "Hardly room for your plate of jelly," smiled the ward orderly, bringing round tea a few moments later.

They left after tea, when Christopher was beginning to look sleepy after all the excitement of the day. In the car park, Mavis said "You haven't opened your present from Father Christmas. Let's see what you have."

Reluctantly, Francesca pulled the parcel from her pocket. She opened the coloured wrapping and revealed a jeweller's box.

"Hm! Jewellery!" Mavis said in surprise. Then she gasped as Francesca lifted the lid to reveal a pair of sparkling earrings. "Those look awfully good ones!" she said. She gave Francesca a curious look. "You didn't *know* him, did you? He's not a friend of yours, is he?"

"How could I know Father Christmas?" Francesca said, laughing. "And how could anyone I knew possibly have known I was going to be at the hospital today?"

"That's true," Mavis said thoughtfully. "I just wondered — well, maybe he had an extra present left over. If he'd given something to one of the parents it might have caused envy."

"I'm sure you're right," Francesca said demurely. She thrust the earrings back into her pocket and started the car for their journey home.

Next morning Francesca lay in bed, luxuriating in a half hour's lie in before getting up. Beside her on the bedside table lay the earrings. They really were beautiful, and the name on the box was that of the town's most exclusive jewellers. Why had he given them to her? And how had he known she would be there? She fingered the box, turning it so that the stones caught the light coming through a chink in the curtain, and flashed fire.

Today she had planned to spend clearing out all her father's personal belongings that previously she hadn't had the heart to disturb. She would sort out his old clothes and all his accumulation of possessions, and then, as soon as the estate agents were open for business again, she would put the house on the market.

She began immediately after breakfast. The clothes went into two piles; those for the local charity shops, and those fit only for discarding altogether. Her father's books, papers, technical instruments and other things, took longer and were more difficult to decide about. Among his drawers she found mementoes that had once belonged to her mother, and there were old photographs of them together which she did not want to keep but couldn't bring herself to destroy.

At mid morning she paused for a cup of coffee and stood, looking out over the little garden. It was bedraggled by winter and the neglect caused by being too busy to tackle the autumn tidying, but the sun was shining and outside it was a beautiful, dry, crisp winter's day.

I've done enough for today, she

thought, draining her cup and surveying the two rows of black bin bags stacked along the floor. One, the things destined for the dustman, was twice as long as the other, to be taken to Oxfam. The table was covered with things, mainly books and photographs, that she had not made up her mind whether to keep.

Francesca fetched her coat, got into her car and drove out of Stonebridge along the road that led to a range of low hills. Her father had loved this part of the countryside. They had often come for walks here together, and he had frequently come alone to think over technical problems. She parked the car off the road at the bottom of a path leading up towards the summit of the nearest hill. The air was cold but she was soon panting with the effort of climbing the steep incline. At the top was an obelisk on a plinth, a memorial to some wealthy, local benefactor from Victorian times.

She reached the obelisk and sat down

on the side of the plinth. From here she could look down over the whole town of Stonebridge and away to the distant hills beyond. The town looked quiet and empty, with few people about on the Bank holiday.

She sat, thinking about Frank, trying to feel his presence beside her. In this place, where he often came, and after a morning of handling his most personal possessions, she felt she ought to be aware of him. She needed him to guide her now.

"Dad, if only I'd been able to speak to you, before — If only I'd been able to say goodbye.," she whispered aloud. "What am I to do? Can I really manage to run Lorrimers by myself? Am I fooling myself to think I can carry on without you? Is it fair to them all to attempt it? Oh, Dad, why did you have to die? I do miss you so!" She closed her eyes against the trickle of tears that threatened to run down her cheeks. "Dad! Help me!" she begged. And there did seem to be something, a sense of someone, strong and comforting, there beside her on the hill. "Help me, please. Tell me what I should do," she said aloud.

A strong arm slipped round her shoulders and a voice said, "Don't fret. I'll do what I can."

This was no ghost of her father. She sprang up, pulling herself out of the embrace, and came face to face with Howard. "What are you doing here?" she demanded angrily.

"I came to find you. I said I'd be in touch with you today." He was leaning against the plinth, dressed in jeans and a leather jacket which looked expensive. He smiled at her. "I telephoned your home but there was no reply so I came to see you. Your car wasn't in the drive so I guessed you might have come here. I knew I was right as soon as I saw it parked at the bottom of the hill."

"You *followed* me here?"

"I didn't need to. This was the place where your father used to come, so I guessed you might come here, too."

"I thought you didn't know my father?"

"I didn't. But this is the favourite place where people come to be by themselves when they want to think. My father used to come up here when he was younger, and in charge of Rutherfords. I was sure your father came here, too."

"Yes, he did. I wish he was here now," Francesca said.

"You miss him a lot, don't you?"

"More than anything I miss not having had the chance to say goodbye. To talk to him about — about what he wanted me to do."

"That's tough," Howard sympathised. "But I'm sure you're doing just what he would have wanted. He expected you to take over when he retired, didn't he?"

"I suppose so. We hardly discussed it. It seemed so far ahead." After a moment Francesca realised that Howard had made a remarkable statement. "But *you* assumed I wouldn't, and most other people did, too."

"I didn't know you then," he said easily, "and I honestly thought you'd want to sell up, that you wouldn't have a clue how to carry on. But you're doing fine. I'm impressed."

Howard, almost on the point of admitting he had been wrong, was an incongruous sight. She stared at him.

"I'd also like to apologise for the other night. It must have been embarrassing for you to have so many people jumping to the wrong conclusion about Lorrimer's future. I assure you, I did nothing to give them reason to think like that, though I suppose the fact that I was with you, fuelled the rumours."

"The local paper was the worst," Francesca said. "They had absolutely no right — "

"They always get things wrong," Howard said soothingly. "Don't let it bother you. It'll all be forgotten by now, anyway." He straightened up from the plinth and put out a hand to her. "Let's walk a bit, shall we? It's too cold to sit for long."

"I wanted to say thank you for the earrings," Francesca said shyly, as they strode along the crest of the hill.

"They were intended as a peace offering, since your evening at the Chamber of Commerce dinner was spoilt," Howard replied. "But don't give me away. They're from Father Christmas and no one's to know differently."

"How did you know I'd be there?"

"Like I said, I called at your home on Christmas Day, but you weren't there. I knew Christopher was in the children's ward and that his mother was your secretary. Didn't take a great deal of deduction to work out you and she might very well be spending Christmas Day together, and you'd both come and see Christopher."

She wanted to ask him about this new side to his life; quite different from the hard-headed businessman which was all she knew of him so far, but he seemed unwilling to say more.

"I wish Father Christmas could have left a present for Lorrimers," she remarked as they walked round the hill and began to turn towards the path downwards again. "We're short of a van. One's in for repair and it won't be ready by the time we open again. I've ordered a new one, but — "

"Why didn't you ask? I can let you have one of ours for a few weeks," Howard said at once. "Rutherfords have a fleet of the things. More than we need at the moment."

"Would you?" She stopped to look at him, relieved but slightly embarrassed as well.

"And a driver too, if you want; but I imagine you've got one kicking his heels anyway."

"It would certainly be a great help." She'd been plucking up courage to ask and was wondering how on earth she was going to admit Lorrimers were stuck without transport.

"I'll see to it first thing when we reopen," Howard said. He gave her a sly smile. "I'll have them cover over the Rutherford name, shall I, so there'll be no confusion if anyone sees it at Lorrimers?"

Francesca was at her desk the morning the factory reopened after the Christmas break when Jim put his head round the door to tell her that a Rutherfords van had been delivered at the loading bay. "Good one, too. Looks practically new," he said. "We're fully mobile now, Miss Lorrimer. Thanks for asking them."

Mavis had called in at the hospital on her way to work and came in to announce that Christopher was being discharged that afternoon. "I talked to the doctor in charge and he said there's no reason why Chris shouldn't start school this term. He would have done normally but I didn't know whether he was strong enough. Chris is delighted; he's been longing to go for months now."

The New Year seemed to hold out the promise of a brighter future for them all. The end of year accounts for Lorrimers were on her desk in front of her and to Francesca's eyes they looked healthy, though her accountant would be able to judge better.

The telephone rang. Howard was on the end of the line. "I've a request," he said. "Will you see the New Year in with me, this year?"

"Well, I — "

"Don't worry. I'm not taking you to some function where people are likely to get any wrong ideas. I thought, just dinner for the two of us and we'll toast the New Year somewhere quiet."

It sounded as if it would suit her mood. She'd finished clearing out everything at the house that she didn't want as part of her new life, but now the place looked bare and rather bleak. She was looking forward to beginning house hunting and planned to see the estate agents at the weekend.

Howard took her to a small, quiet pub out in the country where there were few people but they ate superbly. He drove her there himself and Francesca was relieved that there was no longer the formality of Charters and the big Bentley. Howard owned a Lotus Élan, a superbly comfortable two seater.

When they'd finished their meal it was nearly eleven thirty. Instead of staying on until midnight, he took her out to the car again and turned it towards the hill where they had walked on Boxing Day.

"It's not too cold for a brisk walk, is it?" he asked.

"Up Longbarrow hill? In the *dark*?"

"Not quite in the dark. There's a moon and I have a powerful torch in the back of the car. I want you to come; I've something to show you."

Howard took a small holdall and the torch from the boot of the car, and guided her up the path. It was, in fact, easy to see her way, for the moon was nearly full and the path well-defined. At the top they paused by the obelisk.

"Look!" Howard pointed ahead

towards Stonebridge and Francesca saw the town below them, a myriad of sparkling specks of light in the darkness, like a pile of jewels lying on a misty grey velvet cloth and lit by the moon.

"It's beautiful," she whispered. "I had no idea Stonebridge could look so — so magical."

"Yes, that's the right word. It is magical at night," Howard said softly. "In the daytime it's just a town, but now, with the street lights and the High Street decorated with Christmas lights and the moon giving everything a mysterious shimmer, it could be a fairytale place."

A place where Father Christmas lives, Francesca thought, but she didn't say it. Instead, she said, "I've never been up here at night before."

"Why should you? Not many people would come at this hour." Howard reached down and took something from his holdall. "I thought it would be nice to see the New Year in from up here," he said. "It makes a change from a party or the Town Hall square or wherever most people are. No one would think of here." He turned the torch on and rested it on the plinth. Francesca saw that he had a bottle of Champagne and two glasses he'd taken from the holdall.

"I don't run to an ice bucket but it's cold enough up here," he said, opening it deftly. He poured, and handed her a glass.

"To the future, Francesca. May it prove to be as happy and successful as you dream." As she raised the glass to her lips, they heard the Town Hall clock chime midnight, and as soon as the last stroke faded away, the bells of the parish church in the centre of town rang out a peal to usher in the New Year.

"Happy New Year, Fran!" He bent to kiss her, then carefully taking her glass from her, put them both down beside the bottle and took her in his arms.

She relaxed against him, happy to feel his arms round her. Howard bent his head and his lips touched hers again. "You are becoming very important to me. Do you know that?" he murmured against her hair. "Fran, let's make a New Year resolution to be friends, without any more misunderstandings. Yes?"

Francesca nodded. Her heart was surging with happiness. She was now quite sure that she was in love with Howard. She'd give him her heart, she'd give him anything — but would she ever give him Lorrimers?

5

"YOU certainly look as if you made some New Year resolutions and they're all working out," Mavis said, coming into Francesca's office a couple of weeks later.

"They do seem to be," Francesca replied. "I've put the house on the market, given a spare key to the estate agents and told them to get on with selling it. The business seems to be doing well; the end of year figures were good, even better than Dad predicted last September."

"And your personal life?" Mavis raised an eyebrow.

"I told you. Soon as I know there's a serious buyer for the house, I'm looking for a cottage. Now I'm leaving it, I can admit that I always found that house was rather gloomy. I hope the new owners like redecorating in light colours."

"I didn't mean your move," Mavis said. "I meant your love life. I suppose you'd call it that?"

Francesca sighed. "You're hinting about Howard, I suppose. Well, yes we did go out on New Year's eve and it *was* rather romantic, and yes, I have had lunch in town with him a few times, but we're both busy people. You could hardly describe our friendship as a romance, or even an affair, we just haven't the time."

"But you like him a lot, don't you?"

"Oh, yes, I like him very much. I've changed my opinion of him entirely. He's a really nice person and he genuinely wants Lorrimers to be a success. Clearly, he doesn't want us to be part of Rutherfords any more."

"Are you sure of that? Has he said so? He may want Lorrimers to do well so that it's a better acquisition for him," Mavis warned.

"You are suspicious minded! Don't you like Howard, then?" Francesca demanded.

"I like him well enough; what I've seen of him. But Fran, people like Howard Rutherford are businessmen first and foremost. Do be wary of him. I'm sure he genuinely likes you, but I'm also sure he likes the idea of adding Lorrimers to Rutherfords empire."

"You're quite wrong," Francesca snapped. "I should know what he's like by now and he's gone out of his way to make it clear he has no intention of buying me out. He thought at first I'd be pleased by an offer to sell, as he didn't realise how involved I was with the work. Now he knows better, he's accepted that I won't sell."

Mavis pursed her lips doubtfully. "Be careful, Fran, all the same. He's a charmer; a brilliant businessman and that means he knows how to manipulate people. You won't even be aware — "

"Do you think I'm some naive girl with no experience of men?" Francesca demanded. "I can look after myself perfectly well, thank you and I don't need you to give me advice. Your own experience of men is pretty limited."

Francesca could have torn out her own tongue as soon as she'd spoken, but it was too late. Mavis's lips tightened and she turned away, abruptly leaving the office.

"Mavis, I'm sorry! I — " But Mavis has disappeared into her own office, firmly shutting the door after her.

Francesca considered following to apologise, but hesitated, afraid that saying more might make things worse. Since New Year's Eve on Longbarrow hill, overlooking Stonebridge, she had felt quite differently about Howard. She knew it could be unwise to allow herself to feel too much for him but there was no denying that his manner towards her showed that he was definitely interested in her for herself, not as a route to acquiring her factory. She didn't like the thought that Mavis still mistrusted him; her friend's judgement was something she had respected up to now.

With a sigh, she turned back to the ledger in front of her. This might be the last time she handled this book: the new computer was being installed in a few days and the whole factory records could be put into it. Brought into the twentieth century just in time to greet the twenty first, she thought ruefully.

Suddenly, a loud bang sounded from the machine shop, followed by several shouts. Francesca leapt up and, running from her office, nearly collided with Mavis, also making for the door leading on to the machine shop.

There was a small group of men gathered round one of the machines on the far side. Francesca ran up to them and found Jim.

"Anyone hurt?" she demanded.

"No. Fortunately, no one was touching it and only the operator was nearby. He's shaken, but not hurt. The machine's a mess, though. Look!" Jim pointed. The machine was mangled and buckled; pieces of metal stuck out, twisted into grotesque shapes.

"Whatever happened?" Francesca stared at the machine in horror. If someone had been actually working on it, the consequences could have been horrific.

"Bill here switched on and as soon as the rotating mechanism started up, the whole thing started to crumble," Jim said. "He didn't have time to do anything. He ran to switch off at the mains but the damage had been done by then."

"Does this mean our machines are unsafe? How could any of them behave like this, with no warning?" Francesca asked.

Jim looked grim. "Our machines are all perfectly safe. They're checked and serviced regularly. You know that. This one has been tampered with."

"What?" Francesca looked blankly at him. "How could it have been?"

"I don't know but I'm damn well going to find out." Jim disconnected the current to the machine and pulled forward a toolbox. "I'm going to strip

140

it down, piece by piece, till I find out what went wrong. And I'm warning the men to be particularly careful with all the other machines they use."

Francesca hovered beside Jim as the other workers drifted back to their own work. "Can it be repaired?" she asked.

"Possibly, though I doubt it. There's quite a bit of damage."

"We need this machine. How much to replace it?"

"Couple of thousand. Maybe more. And we'd better replace it soon or orders will be held up." Jim was concentrating on dismantling the machine, his face still thunderous. Francesca left him to it. She and Mavis walked back to their offices, shocked by the incident.

"I'll look up the files; see where and when we bought it," Mavis said. "There's insurance, of course. I'll get on to them straight away."

It was an hour later that Jim knocked on Francesca's office door. He said nothing, but laid a bent and buckled spanner on the desk in front of her.

"Was this — ?" she asked.

"I found it jammed between two cogwheels when I'd opened up the casing. As soon as the machine was started up, that would have been forced between them and caused several parts to buckle, which, in turn, damaged other parts. The proverbial spanner in the works," he added without humour.

"You mean someone was careless enough to leave a spanner there? Or dropped it into the machine?"

"No, I don't. You couldn't drop a spanner into that position, or leave one there by accident. Someone deliberately put it there."

"What?"

Jim sighed. "It's all part of the plan, isn't it? I thought it was very strange when Wentworth's order went missing and turned up later in the old van, but that could be explained by someone's genuine mistake. But the sand in number two van's engine wasn't a mistake and this spanner wasn't either. Someone is bent on sabotage here, Miss Lorrimer. I'm sure of it."

Francesca paled and steadied herself by clutching the desk. "But why, Jim?" she whispered.

"Obvious, I'd say. Someone wants Lorrimers to lose custom. Go out of business, I'd guess. The damage is getting more serious each time. Now, who'd be interested in having that happen, do you suppose?"

"No one on the staff, surely. If we closed down they'd all stand to lose their jobs," Francesca said.

"Maybe. But someone might be being paid for doing this," Jim continued. "Rutherfords wanted to buy you out, didn't they? And if you were bankrupt first, it'd be a lot cheaper and easier to get hold of what would be left."

"No, it couldn't have anything to do with Rutherfords!" Francesca said at once. "They aren't interested any more in buying us out. I'm sure of it."

"Are you? Well, I don't know as I'd be. But I'm going to get to the bottom of this. And our joker has been too clever for his own good, this time. That spanner is evidence."

"You're never looking for fingerprints!"

"No, 'course not. But that's one of our tools. There's a number etched on it and it's listed somewhere in the files Mrs Roberts has in her office. It'll say who it was issued to, and then we'll have the blighter."

"Do you want me to call the police?"

"Wait till I've confronted him with it. I wanted to speak to you first, but I'm on my way to check the tool records."

"You may be only just in time," Francesca pointed out. "Mavis was having a clear out of unnecessary files so that she has only the essentials to put into the new computer. I think we decided the tool records were pointless."

"Not in this case, they aren't." Jim picked up the spanner and crossed the passage to Mavis's office in a couple of strides. Francesca heard him talking to her and then, some moments later, she heard him call, "Thank you very much, Mrs Roberts!" and he strode out towards the machine shop again.

"What was that all about?" Mavis came into Francesca's office. "I'd just thrown out those tool records — he went through torn up bits in the waste paper basket as if he was looking for five pound notes!"

"He says the machine was sabotaged," Francesca said. "He thinks someone is trying to put us out of business."

"I know," Mavis nodded. "And he has his own views about who and why, too."

"That's ridiculous!" Francesca exploded. "Howard wouldn't stoop to anything like that, or let anyone else do it, either."

"Perhaps we'll soon find out," Mavis replied. "Jim found out who that spanner was issued to, and he's gone to find him now."

Moments later, there was a commotion in the passage outside and Jim reappeared, pushing one of the young apprentices before him.

"This is Eric Bostock," he said. "It was his spanner in the machine. Now, you explain to Miss Lorrimer what you thought you were doing, wrecking the thing. You've caused thousands of pounds of damage. Did you know that? And I've no doubt you put sand in number two van's engine, as well. What have you got to say for yourself, then?"

The boy, no more than sixteen, Francesca judged, was plainly terrified. Jim's anger was monumental.

"I didn't do anything, Miss Lorrimer!" He protested. "I never touched that machine! I don't ever work on them. I work on the benches t'other side of the machine shop. Jim knows that."

"It was your spanner. Issued to you when you first started, eight weeks ago. And it wasn't long after you started here that all the trouble began."

Jim shook the boy roughly by the shoulder.

"I lost that spanner! Honest! It went out of my toolkit more 'n a week ago," he spluttered.

"You would say that, of course! Didn't realise it could be traced, did you? Why didn't you report it missing a week ago, then?"

The boy shook his head. "Thought I'd get told off. Made to pay for it," he muttered.

"You may be made to pay for that machine. How would you like that?" Jim shouted at him. "Go on, clear out! I don't want to see you here again!"

"Just a minute, Jim," Francesca intervened. "I'd like to talk to you some more about this. Eric, are you really telling us you had nothing to do with damaging that machine? You didn't lend your spanner to anyone?"

"Why would I want to damage anything, Miss Lorrimer?" Eric appealed to her desperately. "I like it here — it's a good job. I wouldn't risk losing

147

it. I want to train as an engineer; I wouldn't ruin my chances doing damage to things deliberately."

"Not even if you were paid to?" Jim demanded.

Eric stared at him blankly. It was clear he hadn't the faintest idea what Jim meant.

"Eric, go back to work. And take better care of your toolkit in future," Francesca told him.

"You do believe me? I wouldn't do anything like that! Smash up a machine, why, it was awful!" He was still shaking.

"No, I don't believe you had anything to do with it," Francesca said. "But you must admit it looked rather suspicious that it was your spanner."

"I told you. I lost it."

"Go back to work now. But if you do know anything about it, or the damage to number two van, you'd better tell me now, because if I ever find out — "

"I don't! Honest, I don't!"

"Go on, back to work!" Jim gave him a shove towards the door and Eric bolted down the passage and through the connecting door.

"He didn't do it, Jim," Francesca said, looking at Jim's scowling face. "I'm quite sure he didn't."

Jim sighed heavily. "Guess you're right, Miss Lorrimer. Scared rabbit like that wouldn't have it in him. But I want to know who did."

"Shall I telephone the police?" Mavis asked.

"What evidence can we show them? If they come, they'll only disrupt work even more while they swarm over the place and take statements from everybody. No, we'll have to keep a close watch on everyone and everything and hope to catch whoever it is." Francesca looked from Mavis to Jim. "I hate this! Someone here is trying to destroy Lorrimers and everyone is under suspicion until that person is found. I like everyone here, they're all my friends. I hate having to watch them like criminals."

"It couldn't have been an outside job, I suppose?" Mavis asked Jim.

He shook his head. "Place was locked up securely. No sign of a break in. And it had to be someone with a bit of knowledge of that machine to have pushed the spanner in so that no one saw anything until it was switched on."

"Rules me out then." Mavis made a weak attempt at a joke. Jim forced a smile and patted her shoulder. "Guess I over-reacted towards the kid, but I thought I'd got him. When you think about it, stands to reason he wouldn't have used his own spanner. Well, I'll be getting back, Miss Lorrimer. I'm going to ask around if anyone saw anything suspicious, but it's a forlorn hope."

After he'd gone, Mavis hesitated by Francesca's desk. "You're not going to like this, Fran," she said awkwardly, "but young Eric came to us from Rutherfords."

"So?"

"It's just a thought — someone there might have suggested he applied for an apprenticeship here so he could, well, keep an eye on us, serve Rutherford's interests."

"Are you suggesting Howard asked him to smash up parts of our machine shop?" Francesca asked coldly.

"No, of course not. Not Howard. As Managing Director, he'd hardly do such a thing. But someone at Rutherfords might want to help the company acquire Lorrimers at a favourable price. Don't you think so?"

"As I recall," Francesca said, "Eric applied to us because Rutherfords asked him to leave. Wasn't up to their academic standards, he said. He'd hardly be likely to want to do anything for a company who'd given him the sack."

"You've only his word for that," Mavis broke in. "I was looking up his records when Jim found he owned the spanner. Seems we have only his school reference. He told us himself he'd worked at Rutherfords but we've no evidence of what the situation was there."

"I won't believe Rutherfords or any of their staff would stoop to anything so — so criminal," Francesca insisted.

"But why else would someone try to damage Lorrimers?" Mavis persisted. "It doesn't make sense, otherwise. We all stand to lose our jobs — unless someone else takes us over."

Francesca stood up. "I'm going out for a short while," she said abruptly. "If anyone wants me it can wait until I get back, or you can deal with it."

"May I ask where you're going?" Mavis said.

"To Rutherfords, of course! I'm going to speak to Howard and see if I can't clear this matter up straight away." She didn't tell Mavis she was considering asking Howard's advice on how to deal with the situation. Anything I can do to help, you only have to ask, he'd said. He'd loaned them a van when they were desperate and now she felt sure that a confidential talk with him would show her the best way to proceed.

She drove out of Lorrimers car park and turned towards town. Rutherfords was situated on the far side, along the main road out towards the north.

The large, rambling complex of buildings came into view and she turned into the main entrance. A barrier blocked her way and a security guard asked her business.

"My name's Francesca Lorrimer. I'd like to see Mr Howard Rutherford," she told him. Perhaps the name Lorrimer impressed him, for he raised the barrier at once, and directed her to the visitors' car park.

The young lady at the reception desk was not quite so helpful. On learning that Francesca didn't have an appointment, she looked doubtful, but finally agreed to contact Howard's office and speak to his secretary.

"I'm sorry, he's not in his office," she said, looking up from the receiver.

"Could you leave a message?"

"No. I do need to speak to him personally. It's rather urgent; can't he be paged round the building?"

The receptionist went back to her telephone and had a further conversation, turning away so that Francesca could not hear what was being said. Eventually, she put down the receiver and told Francesca, "Someone will come down from Mr Rutherford's office to see you."

This wasn't at all what she wanted, but there was nothing Francesca could do about it. Moments later, the lift doors opened and a smart young woman came towards her.

"Miss Lorrimer? I'm Roz Chapman, Mr Rutherford's secretary. Did you want to see him personally?"

"Yes, I did. It's — it's rather a confidential matter. I really need to speak to him. I can't discuss it with anyone else and I can't leave a message." Francesca looked directly at the young woman, almost daring her to fob her off. Even if his secretary was about the same age as herself, she was only a secretary, not the owner of a company.

Roz looked apologetic and slightly embarrassed. "I'm so sorry, Miss Lorrimer. He's not in his office and we don't know where he is. We can't seem to contact him on his bleeper so I can only think he must have gone home. He was in the office earlier but he left to go to the warehouse. He's not there now, but they haven't seen him since this morning. I can only think he's decided to work from home. He does that sometimes."

"Wouldn't he have told you?"

"Not necessarily. He may have gone home to collect some papers or check on his mail and then decided to stay for a while. He works on projects at home occasionally; there's less likelihood of interruption."

Francesca didn't know whether that last remark was a tactful hint that Howard was not to be disturbed, but it was plain that his secretary really didn't know where he was.

"I'm sure he'll be in tomorrow. Shall I ask him to call you?" she added helpfully.

"Thanks. I'll call him myself," Francesca replied, feeling ungracious.

Back in the car park, she paused before starting up her car again. She really did want to talk to Howard about Eric Bostock and the mysterious things that were happening at the factory. If he was at his home, why shouldn't she go and see him there? She wouldn't take up much of his time, if he was working. It was nearly lunch time and he'd surely take a short break then. Francesca had never been to Howard's home, but she knew where he lived. It was in one of the large, imposing houses overlooking the town: the far side from Longbarrow hill where they'd seen in the New Year together. Stonebridge lay in a hollow surrounded on three sides by low hills and Howard's home was just on the edge of town, at the crest of a hill where wealthy merchants had built their homes in early Victorian times, when the town was beginning to expand and become an important centre for commerce.

She drove out of Rutherford's car park, was deferentially saluted by the security guard, and turned back the way she had come, to drive through town and up the hill to the road known as Ridgemount Avenue.

The houses here were all large and imposing. Some had clearly been turned into flats but there were still several occupied by single families, the well-to-do of Stonebridge. Sir John and Lady Rivers owned a big corner house with a tower, giving a magnificent view of the whole countryside, as well as the town. Howard's home was about a hundred yards further on, not quite so large but equally impressive, with a well-kept drive sweeping round the front of the house. There was no sign of Howard's car, but the drive continued on out of sight round the side of the house, where presumably there were garages.

Francesca pulled up in front of the oak front door and used the heavy knocker. After a few minutes the door was opened by a young woman, perhaps a year or so younger than herself. Francesca had been expecting someone in a maid's cap and apron, even perhaps a butler, and was startled by the girl's appearance. She didn't look like a domestic; her clothes were smart, though not expensive looking, but her high heeled shoes didn't look suitable for housework.

"I'd like to speak to Mr Rutherford, please. Is he at home?" Francesca asked.

The girl looked surprised. "No. He'll be at the factory at this time of day."

"I've just come from there. His secretary said he wasn't in his office and they couldn't contact him anywhere in the building, so they thought he must have come home."

The girl's face broke into a smile. "Oh, silly man! He went off in a hurry this morning and forgot his bleeper. He could be anywhere in that place and no one would be able to find him without it. Did you want him for anything important?"

"It was, rather," Francesca said.

"Well, he'll be somewhere at the factory. If you're going back there, perhaps you could give it to him? I found it slipped down behind the bed this morning. Men are so forgetful, aren't they?" She turned back into the hallway and at that moment a door opened at the far end and a small child came out.

"Mummy!" she called. "Look what I've found!" She waved something in the air and came farther into the hall. "Hello," she said, seeing Francesca. "Look what I've got."

"Trust you to find it!" The girl said, snatching the object from her. "Now she's found Howard's bleeper," she said to Francesca. "Hope she hasn't damaged it. I thought I'd put it out of reach. Do you think you could take

159

it to him, then, if you're going back to Rutherfords?"

"No! I — I mean — I'm not going back there. I — I'll telephone later — " Francesca floundered. Her one thought was to escape from the scene.

"Shall I tell Howard you came? What's your name?" the girl asked, unaware of the havoc her remarks had caused. She picked up the child and held her in her arms. "He's usually home about seven," she added. "Just time to get Madam here in bed and dish up the meal in peace. But you could come back later this evening, perhaps, if the matter's urgent?"

"No! No, I won't be back. It's not important. Don't bother." Francesca backed down the path and fumbled for her car door. Once inside, she started the engine automatically and shot down the drive towards the road. Her one thought was to get away from the house, from the girl who was obviously Howard's wife, and the cosy domestic picture of her standing in the doorway, holding the little girl in her arms and with a surprised, slightly puzzled look on her face.

Francesca drove along the road almost blindly. After a few hundred yards the road joined another, major one at a T junction. Her hands were shaking so much she had to stop and pull in to the side before she reached the junction. She sat, trying to calm down, fighting mixed emotions of anger and misery. Mavis had been right, after all; Howard had been flirting with her solely with the idea of disarming her, planning eventually to persuade her to sell him Lorrimers. The invitations, the romantic evenings, had all been with but one object in mind. He clearly had no personal interest in her — how could he have, with a young wife? Pretty, too, as she grudgingly admitted, and a small daughter of his own?

She tried to think back, over the weeks that had gone by since Howard had first walked into her office with his brash and unexpected request.

He had never actually said he was unmarried, but also, certainly, he'd never mentioned a wife. And the way he had behaved towards her he'd definitely given the impression he was a free man. It might have been an amusing game to him, to let her think he was interested in her for herself and not in the least because she owned Lorrimers. But had he ever thought what her reaction would be? She had taken him at his word and now, too late, she realised that he meant far more to her than mere friendship.

"Damn you, Howard Rutherford!" she said aloud. "Why did you have to be so underhand? You may have succeeded in one way, but I'll see Lorrimers wiped off the face of the earth rather than sell it to you, whatever you offer me!"

Sitting there, the anger and hurt raging in her mind, it was all beginning to make sense. Howard must be thirty at least; most men would be married at that age, particularly those rich enough to afford a beautiful home. And he'd been to her house but never had she been invited to his. There was the initial reaction of the people at the Chamber of Commerce dinner, too. What else could they think, but that theirs was a business relationship if they knew that Howard was a married man?

With a shock, she realised that the day had turned to late afternoon while she had sat in the car, reliving times that had once seemed full of joy and pleasure and now gave so much pain. It was hardly worth driving back to Lorrimers as Mavis would have closed the office and left, yet if she didn't move away from here there was the danger that someone she knew would come round the corner and recognise her. There was nowhere to go but home, and to be thankful she lived on the other side of town, unlikely to meet Howard on the way.

On the way, she considered what she should do. Her first instinct had been to find Mavis and pour out her heart to her closest friend, but Mavis, though she would never say so, would be bound to think 'I told you so'; she had already warned that Howard had ulterior motives for his attentions.

And I was vain enough to think it was me he wanted, Francesca thought bitterly.

Her house had never felt so bleak or empty. She pottered in the kitchen, producing a meal she didn't want and couldn't eat.

Before she went to bed, she'd made up her mind about one thing. It was even more urgent now that she should find a buyer for this house, so that she could move away. Go somewhere new, somewhere Howard would never be invited.

6

IT was hard to put on a brave front and behave normally at work next morning. Not so difficult in front of the factory hands, but Mavis wanted to know what Howard had had to say about Eric.

"I didn't see him. They couldn't locate him at Rutherfords," Francesca said dismissively.

"Why didn't you come back? I was expecting you. There were letters and some cheques to sign and I hate having to leave work over for the next day," Mavis complained.

"I — didn't feel up to it."

"What's wrong? You've been so full of life these last few weeks and now, today, you seem to have had all the stuffing knocked out of you," Mavis continued.

Francesca gave up resisting. "I called

at Howard's house," she said reluctantly. "No wonder he never invited me there. He has a wife and small daughter, a child about the same age as Christopher."

"Oh, no!" Mavis looked stunned. "My dear, I *am* sorry! Oh, I can't believe it! Howard stringing you along and we were all beginning to think — no, I can't believe it of him!"

"There was a young woman and a child there. She was hardly a servant. Called him Howard, and — " Francesca couldn't bring herself to mention the bleeper found behind the bed. There was such an intimate ring to the phrase. "She was clearly a wife, or a live-in girlfriend," she finished.

"Oh, Fran!" Mavis said again, her eyes full of concern.

"You were right all along about him," Francesca said harshly. "I should have listened to you. What else could he have wanted but to ingratiate himself with me so I'd sell out to him? It's what he wanted when he first came into this office and he hasn't changed his mind. I was a fool ever to have been taken in by him."

"Fran — what can I say?"

"Don't say anything. Unless you want to say 'I told you so'. You'd be entitled to."

"I wasn't going to. I was going to be very practical and ask what you were going to do about Eric."

Mavis's business-like tones had a calming effect, bringing Francesca back to realities.

"I don't think he did it," she said. "Jim wants him sacked but I can't bring myself to do that."

"Jim really wants him to be dismissed because he's not terribly bright. I would say that indicated he was innocent, unless he was told to do it by someone else," Mavis said thoughtfully. "And if he did do it, he'd be even more scared than he is now. He'd come out with the full story to try to exonerate himself."

"You may be right. Whatever the situation, it's a horrible feeling,"

Francesca said sadly. "Nobody trusts anyone any more. How can we live like that?"

The week dragged on and on Saturday Francesca went into town to visit the main estate agents. She was studying a display board of properties for sale inside the office when she heard her name called. Turning, she saw Geoff Baxter behind her, clutching a sheaf of property details.

"Hello, Francesca! Remember me?"

"Of course I do! You're looking for a house, too?"

"Flat, actually. I've been living in digs since I came and it's beginning to get me down. I like my job and I plan to stay in Stonebridge so I decided to find myself somewhere permanent. What are you doing? I thought you had a home?"

"Too big," Francesca said with a shrug. "I'm after a cottage somewhere outside the town. Not too far out, but not central."

"Same sort of thing for my flat," said

Geoff. "I say, why don't we look at properties together? You could advise me which are suitable areas. I've a map they've given me and a list of half a dozen possibles, but I don't know where most of these places are."

"Let's go across the Copper Kettle and have a closer look over a cup of coffee," Francesca suggested.

"Good idea! But see what they have that would suit you, first. I can tell you, I'm an expert at spotting dry rot and dodgy repair jobs. Do you want somewhere old and quaint, or small but modernised?"

"I hardly know yet. All I know is I want to move out of my present place."

"A new beginning! I can recommend that. That's what I decided after my wife died, so I came up here when the job of pharmacist was advertised. I'm glad I did. It's no good living surrounded by the past. Even the happy memories become tinged with sadness."

Francesca collected a handful of leaflets describing suitable cottages, and they crossed the road to the town's most popular café.

Before the coffee had been brought, she had marked all the properties on Geoff's map, and he had decided on two places that looked hopeful. There was a cottage for sale round the corner from one of them, and they decided to visit it at the same time. As they drank their coffee and planned their morning, Francesca's spirits rose a little. Geoff was cheerful, encouraging company and it felt pleasant to have someone with her to share her house hunting.

"Shall we go in my car?" she asked, as they finished their coffee and rose to leave.

"I think that might be a good idea," Geoff said gravely. "My car is a bicycle."

As they drove to view the first flat on their list, Geoff told Francesca a bit more about himself. "My wife had a wasting illness. We went all over the country looking for a cure but we were fooling ourselves. It took me a long time to accept that she wouldn't get better and that made it all the harder when she'd gone. But I couldn't wish her back; not to all that suffering."

"My father died suddenly; of a heart attack," Francesca said. "I'd said goodnight to him but he wasn't there in the morning. I've always regretted I was never given the chance to say goodbye. There was so much I wanted to ask him, so much advice he could have given me about Lorrimers, if only we'd known."

"Devastating for you, but better that way for him," Geoff said. "What if he'd become an invalid? From what you've told me, it sounds like Lorrimers was his life. He'd have hated not to be able to carry on working there."

The flat proved disappointing, so, after a cursory look round, they went to the second. This looked more hopeful and Geoff became increasingly enthusiastic as he opened doors and looked out of windows.

"It's the right size and the right location, and the view from the window's terrific," he said. "I like the idea of being high up. Three flights of stairs won't bother me, and there's a shed for the bike at the back. Fran, I think I've found my future home." He took a tape measure out of his pocket and began measuring across the floor and the size of the windows. After a few minutes he stopped, looking at her contritely.

"I'm sorry. I forgot we were looking for a place for you, too. This can wait; come on, let's see if you can be as lucky with your place."

The cottage round the corner was hopeless, and two others they visited were not what Francesca had in mind, either. "Never mind; I've plenty of time. I still have to sell my present house first," she said. "Do you want to go back to the estate agents and tell them you'll have that flat?"

Geoff nodded. "Yes, better clinch it

now before someone else comes along. I've got to think about furniture, too. I sold most of mine when I came up here. Care to help me choose some?"

"I still have the weekend groceries to buy," Francesca excused herself.

Geoff looked apologetic. "Sorry, I was monopolising your time and you've precious little to spare, with your commitments. But could I ask you — as a thank you for helping me find my flat — would you have dinner with me, tonight?"

"Thank you, Geoff. That would be very nice." He was a pleasant, undemanding companion and the thought of being taken out to dinner by him, was soothing to her still wounded feelings. It was nice to know she wouldn't have to spend another evening alone with her thoughts about Howard, reliving those awful moments on the doorstep of his house.

She shopped for the coming week, dropped into the estate agents to return a few keys, then went home for a leisurely bath before meeting Geoff again later that evening.

They went to an Indian restaurant in the High Street and Francesca, who had never eaten authentic Indian food before, discovered that she enjoyed it. It was, apparently, one of Geoff's great passions. He was in high spirits, having made a firm offer for the flat and been told it was almost certain to be accepted. There was no chain, fortunately, being an executor's sale, so he would be able to move in as soon as contracts had been signed.

"You'll be my first guest to be invited to my flat warming," he told her. "But you'll have to sit on the floor unless I've bought some chairs first."

They left the restaurant just as the Town Hall clock was striking ten. "Care for a drink before closing time? It's a bit early to go home yet," Geoff invited.

"No, thanks. I'm too full."

"Let's stroll up the High Street to walk it off," he suggested. "Do some window shopping on the way. There's a large furniture store halfway along on the other side; we can see what they have."

Francesca laughed. "You're determined to have me choose your furniture for you! Have you no opinions of your own? If you're not careful, I'll try to sell you my own houseful. I have far too much for a cottage." To her amusement, she was rewarded by a look of horror on Geoff's face.

"Only joking. My stuff's terribly old-fashioned. I wouldn't wish any of it on anyone."

They wandered along the High Street in good spirits. The town was deserted, most people either already home, or not yet leaving the pubs or the one cinema.

"There's a soft furnishings display!" Geoff said suddenly, pointing across the road. "I need curtains! I'll see what they have." He ran across the road and Francesca was about to follow more slowly when a car came cruising down the street between them. It slowed as it passed her and she recognised it as Howard's Lotus Elan. There was nothing she could do; it was too late to step back into a shop doorway, he'd already seen her. He drew up beside her and leaned across the passenger seat, lowering the window.

"Hello, Fran!" He greeted her. "I didn't expect to see you wandering round the town at this time of night! Can I give you a lift anywhere?" If he'd noticed Geoff, clearly he hadn't realised they were together.

"No, thank you," Francesca replied as freezingly as she could. "And why shouldn't I walk round the town if I choose, at any time of the day or night?"

Howard looked taken aback. "Well, no reason, of course." Then, as if he'd seen a reason for her sharpness, said "You were looking for me the other day, I believe? My secretary told me you'd been to the factory but they couldn't locate me. I was at the back of the building with our architect and hadn't brought my bleeper. I'm so sorry I didn't get back to you. What did you want? Was it important?"

"It doesn't matter," Francesca snapped. "Any business matters between us can be dealt with by letter. I doubt there will be anything other than business that I'd wish to contact you about."

"What, exactly, does that mean?" Howard asked, genuinely puzzled.

"It means that I have no wish to have anything further to do with someone who — who is a philanderer, an utter womaniser!" Francesca said furiously.

Howard looked astonished. Then he grinned and said, "Oh, you mean this gorgeous redhead I have here beside me?" indicating the empty car seat. Francesca was about to reply when Geoff came back, crossing the road behind the car so that neither she nor Howard noticed him until he said, "You coming across to see, Fran? There are some curtains just right for the bedroom. Come and tell me what you think." He bent down to peer into the car. "Oh, hello, Rutherford," he remarked easily. "Fran and I have been looking at flats this afternoon. Just been to the Indian place for a meal. Sorry if I'm breathing curry over you."

Howard said nothing, but he stared at Francesca for a long moment. Then he said coldly, "I see of course that you have no need of a lift. My apologies for accosting you." He moved back into the driving seat and the car shot away in one smooth movement, leaving Francesca staring open-mouthed after him.

"Oh, dear, did I drop a brick?" Geoff said. "I have a feeling I might have phrased that a little better."

"It doesn't matter," Francesca said dully. "Mr Rutherford is just another local factory owner. It doesn't matter what he thought then."

But it did matter. He'd looked — hurt, when he'd seen that Geoff was with her. But what right had he to feel like that when he'd been two-timing her with a wife at home?

The following week the computer system arrived and was installed. Mavis, who had expressed nervousness about it and fear that she'd never learn to master it, or would lose vital records, suddenly discovered that it was simpler than she'd expected and that it would halve her workload once the files had been transferred.

"If I'd known it was like this I'd have persuaded your father to have one, long ago," she said to Francesca enthusiastically. "I put him off, I'm afraid. We spoke about it several times, but I said I was happy with things as they were. I should have known better. Do you know they even have a computer at Christopher's school? He'll be able to tell me what to do if I have problems."

On Wednesday the bank telephoned. Mavis took the call and spoke to Francesca. "Mr Anderson says he wants to see you urgently. Can you make an appointment with him for this afternoon?"

"The overdraft!" Francesca gasped. "He gave it to us for three months. It *can't* be due for repayment already! Can he call it in early, do you suppose?"

"No idea. You'd better see him and find out," Mavis said unhelpfully.

"What did he sound like? Friendly? Stern? Smug?"

"I only spoke to his secretary. She said it was urgent, so I made an appointment for half past two and said I'd confirm it. All right with you?"

Francesca nodded. Half the morning would now be spent worrying, but she had work to do and couldn't drop everything straight away.

Mr Anderson gave nothing away when he greeted her in his office later. He had a bulging file lying open in front of him and he consulted some papers in it before he looked up at her, clasped his hands under his chin and peered at her over the top of his spectacles.

"And how is Lorrimers progressing these days?"

Francesca gulped. "We're doing quite well. Orders have always picked up in the spring. We had a slight hiccup — damage to a machine. It held us back for a short while but it's repaired now." She wasn't going to tell him it had been deliberately damaged. He'd wonder, as she frequently did now, what was going to happen next and whether the unknown saboteur would eventually cause damage that would put Lorrimers out of action permanently.

"You had some rather ambitious building plans, as I recall," Mr Anderson prompted. "Any more thoughts about that?"

He wants me to admit I was ridiculously naive to think I could start on Dad's long-term dream so soon, Francesca thought resentfully. "I still have hopes of building a canteen and staff room for my workers," she said. "But I recognise that I'm not in a position to do anything like that for some time yet. The main building is shabby; it needs some refurbishment and that's a priority."

Mr Anderson nodded, his face expressionless. "You have an overdraft at present, I believe?"

"Yes, but that was for three months. There's still three weeks to run and I have made arrangements for paying it off on a regular basis," Francesca replied. She was all too well aware that, if he chose, Mr Anderson could make things very difficult for her. She couldn't bear the feeling of his playing cat and mouse with her, and burst out, "Why have you asked me to come and see you, Mr Anderson? Is there some problem? Does the bank want its money back, all of it, right now?"

Mr Anderson laughed. Well, it was as near to a laugh as he would permit himself. "My dear young lady!" he exclaimed. "No, no, it's nothing like that. Have you forgotten that at our last meeting I suggested that to raise sufficient capital for your long-term plans, Lorrimers needed a backer, someone to invest in your company? Well, I think I have found just such a person for you."

"What?" Francesca stared at him, dumbfounded. This was the very last thing she had expected.

"I told you I would make enquiries, but at the time I didn't hold out much hope of success. But I've had an approach from someone who is interested in making a long term investment and wants to consider a small manufacturing company with growth potential. He decided that Lorrimers would be a good choice." He mentioned a sum which made Francesca gasp.

"Who is he, this person who wants to invest that much in my company?" She asked.

"Ah. Unfortunately, I am not at liberty to divulge his name. Any dealings would be through this bank, but you have my solemn assurance that it is a perfectly genuine offer. The money is there, there is no question of any underhand dealing. I will have the forms drawn up — "

"It's Howard Rutherford, isn't it?" Francesca broke in.

"I beg your pardon?"

"It's Howard Rutherford who wants to invest in my company," Francesca said angrily. "It's his way of getting hold of it entirely eventually. I've refused to sell out to him and so he's thought of this way of getting control before I've realised what's happening. Well, no thank you. I don't want his money. I'd sooner struggle on and do without than accept. I want nothing to do with that man, or his money."

"My dear young lady!" Mr Anderson said again, his bland expression changing to one of astonishment at her outburst. "Do you know what you are saying? You are refusing financial help out of hand and you surely cannot appreciate that this is a golden opportunity you have been offered, something I did not expect and something that may not come your way again. Do, please, consider what it means and don't be so rash as to reject it in this way."

"If the money comes from Howard Rutherford I don't want it," Francesca said stubbornly.

Mr Anderson looked bewildered. "I don't understand you," he said. "This investment could be the turning point in Lorrimer's future. But without it, your company might very well cease trading within a year or so. Have you considered what that could mean to your workforce? Not a large one, I know, but there will certainly be several who will find it difficult to obtain alternative employment in Stonebridge. Married men, with responsibilities and dependents. Are you prepared to gamble with their future security for what appears to me to be an extraordinary objection?"

Francesca flushed. Put like that, it sounded as if she was being incredibly selfish. Once again, she had to face the fact that if Lorrimers couldn't carry on, it would be better for her staff if they were taken over by someone like Rutherfords than be made redundant with no guarantee of future work.

"Can you tell me that this backer *isn't* Howard Rutherford?" she asked.

"I cannot discuss his identity at all, except to say the bank has investigated his credentials and can assure you that it is a bona fide approach. He is solvent and everything is completely above board." Mr Anderson unbent a little to add, "If you are so concerned to know if it is Mr Rutherford, then perhaps you should try the direct approach? Why don't you ask him yourself? He may be willing to satisfy your enquiry."

She could hardly do that. She'd vowed never to have anything to do with the man, ever again. But was she letting her personal feelings intrude into her business world, and doing unnecessary damage? Frank had often said it was necessary to put one's private opinions aside and do business, even be helpful and friendly, to people one didn't like. She was not being a good businesswoman in letting her feelings take over.

"Please tell your client, whoever he is, that I'd be glad to accept him as an investor," she told Mr Anderson stiffly. "And perhaps you'll deal with the details for both of us? You know that I am relying on you to keep a watch on things. Lorrimers is mine and I don't want *anyone* gaining enough power through investment to be able to take over my company, or have more authority than I have."

Mr Anderson nodded wearily. "I can assure you, Miss Lorrimer, that that is not the case. My client is interested only in a good return for his money; for capital appreciation. He has assured himself of your company's potential but he is certainly not interested in interfering in its management. If, of course, he thought it was poorly managed, he would withdraw his money. It's as simple as that."

Francesca left the manager's office

with mixed feelings. Who but Howard could be wanting to invest in Lorrimers? And what other reason would he have than a plan to gain control eventually? But it was true that she needed this money. With it, she could do so much to improve her factory. Forewarned was forearmed, she told herself. She'd take Howard's money but she'd make sure he never had the chance to take Lorrimers in exchange.

Mavis was anxiously waiting to hear about the interview.

"It must be Howard!" Francesca said, "Only he would think up a scheme like this."

"It needn't be," Mavis replied. "The bank said they'd look out a backer for you and Howard isn't the only rich man in Stonebridge, or even the richest. It could be anyone. A London businessman, even, wanting an investment. I should imagine it's standard practice not to divulge names; don't read too much into that."

"I feel it's the kind of thing Howard

would do," Francesca said. "And he'd never do it out of the goodness of his heart. That man has no heart."

"You're getting paranoid about that man," Mavis said severely. "So, he took you to a dinner dance and forgot to mention he'd left a wife at home. But it *was* a semi-business occasion, to introduce you to the useful people of Stonebridge, wasn't it? And it's helped, hasn't it? And he lent us the van, which, by the way, our driver returned last Friday. Has he really been that terrible?"

Not if she'd taken his flirtations as lightly as he had, Francesca admitted to herself. Had she really been so naive as to misinterpret all his actions? Had she been so sure he was becoming seriously interested in her for herself, just because she wanted to believe it?

"I'm not the first, and I don't suppose I'll be the last, to become involved unwittingly with a married man," she said, shrugging her shoulders. "It's that I didn't realise the experience could be so painful."

Mavis put an arm round her friend's shoulders. "Poor love! I hadn't realised — Look, come and spend the evening with Chris and me. You shouldn't be by yourself in that big house of yours every evening. We can eat some horrible, calorie-laden junk food for supper and then play silly board games afterwards. Chris will love it and we'll behave like children again."

Francesca smiled. "Whatever would I do without you, Mavis?"

"You'd have to get a secretary who really knows how to work your wretched computers!" Mavis quipped, returning to her office.

The evening was a success. For a few hours Francesca forgot her heartache over Howard. What did it matter that he'd decided to invest in Lorrimers, if indeed it was he? She still owned her father's company and she was determined to keep things that way.

7

LIFE continued relatively smoothly over the following weeks. Various improvements to the factory were put in hand and Francesca was thinking seriously about her father's plans for a staff canteen. If things continued well, she would be able to tell the builders to start work on it in the near future.

She'd seen nothing of Howard since the evening she'd spent with Geoff. She hadn't heard much from Geoff, either, though she knew he'd now moved into his new flat. There had been an invitation to his house-warming party a couple of weeks ago, but she hadn't gone; pleading that she was too busy at work. That was partly true, but the real reason was that she was hesitant now about making any friendships with men. Howard had made her wary and distrustful. She resented him for it, but the feeling was there, none the less.

It was mid-February, one of the coldest nights of the year, when the disaster struck. She had spent the evening with Mavis and Chris, as she often did nowadays, and arrived home late, to find her house cold and depressingly unwelcoming. The search for a cottage had ground to a halt since the first week of the year. No one was moving house at this season, and the cottages on offer were not what she wanted; buildings long empty and hard to sell, for good reason.

Francesca considered lighting the fire, but it seemed pointless at that hour. She switched on her electric blanket and then made herself a cup of tea to give it time to warm up. Wandering around the kitchen, she came across a book she had begun reading and forgotten, and became absorbed in it again. In spite of the cold, it was nearly an hour later before she realised what she'd done, emptied the pot of stone-cold tea into the sink and went upstairs to an extremely warm and now very inviting bed.

The result was that she slept heavily. She was dreaming about being at the factory, trying to tell Mavis something but always being interrupted by the telephone. As Mavis ran to answer the machine on her desk, her own began ringing. It continued ringing even after she'd picked up the receiver. There seemed to be no one at the other end, just a continuous ringing sound that wouldn't stop.

She struggled to a half awake state, and the telephone in her dream continued to ring. At last it penetrated her befuddled senses — it was not part of her dream, the telephone in the hall downstairs was ringing for real; must have been ringing for some minutes.

Francesca stumbled out of bed and the cold hit her. She thrust her feet into her slippers and reached for her dressing gown, regretting that neither she nor Frank had considered a bedside extension.

"Why am I doing this? It's bound to be a wrong number," she muttered. "Should have stayed in bed. No one could possibly — "

She picked up the receiver, almost surprised that, unlike in her dream, the ringing stopped. As she put it to her ear she thought she heard a faint, muffled voice say "At last!"

"Who is it?" she demanded crossly.

"Miss Lorrimer?" The answering voice was masculine and brisk. He sounded very wide awake. "I understand you are the owner of Lorrimer's Engineering, on the Chester Road?"

"Yes, but why are you ringing me at this hour? Do you realise it's three in the morning?"

"Yes, Madam. I'm sorry to disturb you. This is Inspector Beavis, Stonebridge police here. There's some trouble at the factory."

"Trouble? What kind of trouble?" Instantly, she was wide awake.

"There's a fire been reported. I think you should come to the premises as soon as you can. The fire brigade has been called. They'll be there by now but they'll need you to tell them if there are any inflammable materials stored there, and to open the premises — I assume you have a set of keys?"

"Yes, yes, I have keys." She reached for them automatically as she spoke. She always left her set of factory keys on the shelf below the telephone ledge.

"Shall I send a squad car to pick you up? It can be at your house in ten minutes."

"No, I'll drive there myself. I'm not even dressed." She was conscious she was still clutching her dressing gown round her shoulders.

"It would be advisable to come as soon as possible, Miss Lorrimer," the Inspector urged, then added with a human touch, "put something warm on, it's a bitter night, Miss."

Francesca put down the receiver in a daze. A fire at Lorrimers! How serious, she wondered. The Inspector hadn't said, but clearly serious enough to require her presence as soon as possible.

She ran upstairs, pulled on jeans and her thickest sweater, her walking boots and anorak and wound a scarf round her neck. She was out of the house in five minutes flat, getting the car out of the garage and willing herself to stay calm so that she would at least drive safely.

The streets were completely deserted. In the distance she heard the sound of an alarm bell, but whether it was a police car or another fire engine, she couldn't tell.

She saw the glow as she turned into the main road that led to the factory, half a mile further on. As she drew nearer, she saw the flickering of flames. The roof seemed to be alight at the front of the building. A policeman waved her down some two hundred yards from the site.

"Can't go on, I'm afraid, Miss."

"I'm Francesca Lorrimer. I own the factory. I've brought keys — " She waved them in the Constable's face.

"You'll have to pull over to the side of the road and walk. Must keep this area clear for the appliances," he told her. "Thanks for coming so promptly, Miss Lorrimer. I'll take the keys to the Fire Chief and tell him you're here. He'll be wanting to speak to you about the layout of the building and what stores you have."

Francesca parked by the side of the road and walked towards the blazing building. The roof and the building frame were metal, but they had been repaired and reinforced since the time it had been an aeroplane hangar, and there were wood beams where a false ceiling had been put in for extra storage space.

The sight that met her as she reached the edge of the factory car park was like a surreal painting. The fire brigade had set up floodlights to help them see to fight the blaze, and the whole place was bathed in a strange, greenish light. The fire engines were drawn up on the parking space, each with a hose directed at the flames, which flickered on the roof, giving the building the appearance of a halo of fire all round it. There were police cars drawn up at the side and, discreetly in a corner, an ambulance. Francesca stood watching, still numb with shock and unable to take in what she was seeing.

A man approached her from the group of firemen. "Miss Lorrimer?"

She nodded.

"I'm Fire Chief Bryan Chandler. We had a report about half an hour ago from a passing motorist that he could see smoke and smell burning. It's broken out on the roof since then, but it appears to be restricted to that area and the side. What's to the right of the building?"

"The offices. My office, and my secretary's. There are all the company's records and the new computer system, and — oh, no!" Francesca broke off.

"We were in the middle of transferring our records on to the computer. If the office is on fire, I've lost both sets of records — all my customers' names, all the records of accounts sent out — "

The fireman took her arm. "Better sit down, Miss Lorrimer. I'll take you over to one of the police cars. I've questions to ask, but not standing here."

In the darkness of the police car's interior, Francesca struggled to answer the Fire Chief's questions. Yes, they did keep some inflammable materials on the site, but mainly at the back of the building, which had escaped the flames so far. There were the vans, too, and a certain amount of diesel for their use.

"As far as we can tell at this stage, the fire seems to have started in the side building attached to the factory," the fireman said. "A wooden frame structure. Those are your offices, you say? When were you there last?"

"This evening. I left about six o'clock." Francesca still stared at the blazing building.

"Were you the last to leave? Who else was there?" The questions were searching.

"Usually only my secretary, Mavis Roberts, and I are there, but the men come in and out from time to time. There's a communicating door to the main shopfloor. Mavis and I left together this evening. I think everyone had left the other part of the building by then. It seemed quiet. Our foreman, Jim Donovan, might still have been there. He has a small office on the far side where he does his paperwork."

"Who locked up, then?"

"I locked up the offices. Jim has his own set of keys. But he might not have been there — he doesn't always stay on. It depends on the work." She was getting confused. "You said the fire started in the offices? How could that be? There's nothing that could ignite. Neither of us smokes, and we had the wiring checked before the computer terminals were installed."

The Fire Chief shrugged. "We'll find out more once the flames have been dowsed and we can get in and examine everything properly. Lucky you had a metal roof or there wouldn't be much left. Those metal sheets have buckled in the heat, of course."

"What about the main building? Has the fire taken hold there, too? There's so much smoke I can't see anything," Francesca asked.

"Not as bad as it looks, from what we can tell at this stage. The fire went from the wooden office structure, up the wall to the roof, but only a wooden ceiling there seems to have ignited. Worst damage will probably be the roof crashing down on to the plant below, and subsequent water damage, but that's inevitable. Excuse me, Miss Lorrimer, but I must get back to my men. I'd advise you to stay inside the car. It's safer, and you can do nothing further."

Francesca nodded, hardly aware that the Fire Chief had opened the door and stepped outside. She went on staring at the blazing building, seeing the black outlines of moving figures bringing up the hoses, silhouetted against the light.

She wasn't aware of time passing, but eventually someone tapping on the window caught her attention and she opened the door.

"Miss Lorrimer — are you all right? They said you were sitting in a police car." It was Jim Donovan, trousers pulled on below what looked like a pyjama jacket top; a scarf wound round his neck but no coat.

"Jim! Come and sit with me. You must be frozen." She reached out a hand and pulled him inside.

"The police rang me. What happened? How long have the fire brigade been here? How did it start?"

"I don't know the answer to any of those questions," Francesca said. "They said a passing motorist gave the alarm. We should be grateful to him, I suppose, otherwise it could have burnt for hours before anyone knew anything about it. They say they think it started in the office, but I can't see how it possibly could. Come to that, I don't see how a fire *could* have started anywhere in the building. All the staff are very safety conscious. And if someone *had* left a smouldering cigarette end it wouldn't have been in the offices."

Jim looked grey with concern and lack of sleep, but his face was grim. "I'm wondering," he muttered. "Is this another spanner in the works?"

"What do you mean?" Francesca was afraid she already knew what he meant.

"It's too soon to say, but I was wondering — what was Eric doing yesterday?"

"Oh, no! Not Eric! He wouldn't!"

"Someone deliberately put a spanner in that machine. We got it going again, so maybe whoever it was, decided to do something more drastic."

"Jim, I'm sure you're wrong. It must be an electrical fault. Perhaps the computer overloaded the system, or someone left an electric kettle on, or something like that." Francesca refused to let her mind consider Jim's suggestion.

They stayed in the police car for nearly two hours, then the Fire Chief reported that the blaze was largely under control.

"Most of the flames are out. We'll wait till it's cool enough to go in, then check on the damage and see if we can find the cause. There's no point in your staying any longer, Miss Lorrimer. We'll be here for another hour or so, clearing up, but there's nothing for you to do. One of the policemen will drive you home."

"I have my car — " Francesca began.

"I'll drive you home in it, if you like," Jim broke in. "You don't want to drive yourself, do you?"

In truth she didn't. She still felt shaky as he helped her out of the police car. "What about you getting home?" she asked.

"I'll walk," he replied. "I need some fresh air after all that smoke. And I need to marshal my thoughts."

Francesca didn't argue with him. She needed to collect her own thoughts too and they barely spoke on the journey back to her house.

As he left her, Jim said "I'll telephone the staff, tell them not to come in this morning, since there's little point. But I imagine by lunch time the firemen will be finished and we can muster for a clear up; see what the damage really is, and how much we can keep going."

Francesca nodded. "Thanks, Jim. That would be very helpful. I'm in such a daze I don't know what to do next."

"Have a cup of tea, and maybe a few hours' sleep," Jim advised. "I know everyone's telephone numbers so I'll call from home. They'll be just about ready to leave by the time I get to them." He hesitated, then said,

"Perhaps you could ring Mrs Roberts, though? It'll be a shock to her and maybe it would be better, coming from you . . . ?"

Francesca nodded in understanding. "Yes, of course I'll ring her. Do you think I should mention that they think the fire started in the offices?"

"She'll have to know that, sometime. But perhaps it might be better to wait until we know more details. Mrs Roberts is so conscientious, she might worry it was something she had done, though that's very unlikely."

Francesca thanked Jim again and let herself into her house. After the excitements of the night she felt exhausted, but too keyed up to consider going back to bed. She telephoned Mavis, who was already up and half dressed, in spite of the early hour.

"What happened?" she gasped, when Francesca told her the bare details. "Would you like me to come over to your house?"

"Yes, please. We'll need to talk

about what we're to do, though I suppose we can't do that until we know exactly what the damage is."

"Insurance policies?" Mavis said. "I remember your father saying he kept them at the bank, just in case something like this ever happened. He made a little joke about the place burning down — " Mavis's voice broke, and she said, "I'll call at the bank on my way. Your father made me a signatory for collecting and depositing Lorrimer's papers. I'll bring everything with me." She put the receiver down and so did not hear Francesca's reply, "Mavis, you're truly a treasure." Her father had clearly thought so. Francesca has always known how highly Frank had always regarded Mavis. "Without Mavis Lorrimers would fall to pieces in a month," he'd often said. It had been a sort of family joke between them, every time there had been a problem Mavis had managed to solve in her quiet, efficient way.

Now, Francesca was beginning to believe it might, quite literally, be true.

Mavis arrived at half past ten, laden with papers from the bank. "I'll sort through these and find the policies," she said, settling herself at the dining room table.

"I'll make you some coffee," Francesca offered, feeling there was nothing much else she could do.

She had hardly put the kettle on when her doorbell rang. On the step were two men, serious-faced. Though they were not in uniform, their build and general manner proclaimed police.

"Miss Lorrimer? I'm Detective Inspector Stannard and this is Inspector Baker from the Fire Investigation Department. May we come in and speak to you, please?"

Francesca stepped back to let them in. She noticed that Inspector Baker was carrying something in a plastic bag, incongruously showing the logo of the town's biggest supermarket.

She showed them into the sitting room and offered coffee, which they refused.

"We've found the cause of your fire," said Detective Inspector Stannard.

"That was quick! I'd hardly have thought you'd be able to get inside yet."

"The office section was burnt out, being largely wooden. That was clearly where the fire had started, so it didn't take long to examine that area. Tell me, do you know what this is?"

Inspector Baker put down his plastic carrier bag as he spoke, and drew from it something wrapped in thick, plain plastic. When he unwrapped that, Francesca saw a blackened, misshapen lump of what looked like metal, or plastic, about the size of a football. There were slight flecks of red on it, as if the object had been that colour originally.

"What on earth is it?" she asked.

"You don't recognise it? We found it in a corner of one of the offices.

It is, or rather, was, before the fire, a petrol can."

"A what?" she gasped.

"A petrol can. There's clear evidence that someone sprinkled the contents of this round both offices, and dowsed the connecting door. Then they threw the empty can away before setting light to the place."

"Then — then it really was deliberate? Arson!" Francesca gasped.

"Why do you say it like that, Miss Lorrimer?" Detective Inspector Stannard said sharply. "Have you any reason for thinking this fire might have been arson?"

"Well, no, not exactly. Expect that we have had one or two rather strange things happen lately," Francesca said unwillingly. "Someone trying to damage our reputation, or hold up production. Just silly things, annoying but not as serious as this."

"Did you report any of these incidents to the police?" Stannard asked.

"No. They were just — well, we

weren't sure they weren't mistakes, or accidents. Looking back now I realise they must all have been deliberate attempts to damage the factory."

"You'd better tell us all about them. We shall have to see if there's some connection between all the incidents," Stannard said. He sighed gustily as he took out his notebook and Francesca had the feeling he thought she was very remiss for not reporting the damaged van and the spanner in the machine when they had been discovered.

The two men stayed nearly an hour, taking a full statement from her. Francesca did not voice any of the suspicions she and Jim had had about who might have been responsible. Nor did she mention Howard Rutherford and his obsession to add Lorrimers to his empire. It seemed too far-fetched an idea to suggest to these investigators, and, besides, whatever the truth, she could hardly imagine Howard himself throwing petrol around her office and setting it on fire.

After they'd finally gone, she and Mavis had a quick sandwich lunch before setting off to see what could be salvaged from the factory building. As they were leaving, the telephone rang.

"Francesca, my dear! I've just heard the news! I'm stunned! I'm most terribly sorry!" It was Howard on the end of the line.

"Are you?" she said, dully.

"I rang to ask — is there anything I can do to help? If you need room to store anything, there's plenty of space at Rutherfords — "

The strain of the last few hours was proving too much for her, and Francesca snapped.

"Haven't you done enough already?" she stormed. "You've been trying for months to stop me running my business, one way or another. Now I suppose you think you've succeeded. Well, you haven't! I don't want any help from you, ever! I'll succeed on my own terms and in spite of you!" She banged the receiver back on to its rest.

"Was that wise?" Mavis asked mildly.

"I'm convinced Howard is behind everything that's gone wrong at Lorrimers," Francesca said angrily. "He's wanted me out, ever since Dad died. He's such a chauvinist he can't bear the idea of a woman running a business successfully."

"He never struck me as a chauvinist," Mavis said. "Fran, I think you are beginning to be paranoid about that man. Why do you hate him so much?"

"I don't hate him. I wish I could." Francesca looked forlornly at her friend. "I liked him a great deal. In fact, he was beginning to be very important to me. That's the trouble. I believed it was me, not Lorrimers, he wanted, but I was wrong. That man would stop at nothing to get what he wants. He'd even let down his wife and child to achieve his aims. He's a rat, but I suppose it's rats that have all the attraction. I think the truth is that I'm so angry with him because I'm really angry at myself. I can't get him out of my system. I'm like the original little innocent who fell for a charming philanderer, who's also a con man. I just wish — oh, Mavis, I just wish he'd been fat, balding and middle-aged! I could cope with his scheming far better if I hadn't fallen in love with him."

When they arrived at Lorrimers they found Jim organising a clean up in the machine shop, clearing away fallen debris from the roof and water damage from the fire brigade. The firemen had gone, but they had made sure there would be no resurgence of the flames by soaking everything with their hoses.

"No electrical power, of course," Jim greeted them. "Once things have dried out I'll get the electricians on to repairs. The machines don't seem too bad, apart from water damage. We can strip most down and dry them out. Half the roof's gone. I've got on to a roofing company who are coming to rig up a temporary cover. Perhaps you should take the opportunity to think about something other than the corrugated roof."

"How badly is the building damaged?" Mavis asked.

"The main factory isn't too bad. Your office and Miss Lorrimer's are completely gutted and I'm afraid there's not much to salvage from them. But there's one amazing thing; your old filing cabinets withstood the heat and though they're buckled, the contents look usable. You may find you have your files largely intact, after all."

"Extra good quality, fire-proof cabinets," Mavis said with a broad grin on her face. "Your father paid good money for them years ago, Francesca, and it's paid off. I suppose the computer has been completely destroyed?"

They did what they could to restore order, but there was not much that could be done in a freezing, roofless shell. Francesca almost regretted her outburst to Howard earlier. Some storage space, or basic office equipment and a room and telephone where Mavis could work would have been a help, but she could hardly go back and ask him after what she'd said to him.

The police called again with more questions that evening. There had been a witness who said she had seen a youth running along the road, away from the site, some time before the fire had been reported. There was no description, and the whole story was vague. Francesca was asked if there was anyone she thought might have a grudge against her or Lorrimers, or if she had any reason to suspect anyone of arson. It was a difficult question; she didn't want to mention Eric because she couldn't really believe he had had anything to do with damaging the machine, though she knew Jim still had serious doubts about the youth. Neither could she mention Howard. What on earth would the police make of it if she accused the managing director of the largest business in Stonebridge of arson and wilful damage? They'd think her mad. Of course, she didn't imagine Howard had done anything himself, but surely he must be behind all this? There didn't seem any other explanation.

"I don't know of anyone who would actually set fire to the factory," she said hesitantly. "There were people who didn't approve of a woman, especially someone of my age, taking over the place when my father died. But that's not the same thing as trying to destroy the place."

"You told us there were other incidents which looked like deliberate damage," the policeman persisted. "Any idea who might have been responsible for those?"

"We could never be certain. My foreman identified a spanner that was dropped into a machine, but anyone could have picked it up."

The policeman closed his notebook, sighed and stood up. "We're investigating this report of a youth seen near the place about half an hour before the fire was reported, but I don't hold out much hope. It was one of the local doctors, in fact, driving out to see a patient. She noticed the lad, she said, because she was surprised to see someone in that area at around two in the morning. There are no houses nearby. She said she'd have offered him a lift if she hadn't been going to a call, and at the time her mind was on her patient — a serious, suspected heart attack, I understand, so she didn't pay any attention to what he looked like."

Somehow, Lorrimers became operational again in the next few weeks. The roof was repaired, but Francesca began to think about the possibility of a new building. Aircraft hangars weren't intended to last forever and this one had been there since the Second World War; high time it was replaced. With the insurance money and the money the unknown investor had contributed, they could certainly make a start. Just so long as nothing else happened to threaten Lorrimer's future.

She heard no more from the police and assumed they hadn't been able to trace the mysterious youth. The workforce were all interviewed but nothing of any significance resulted. There was no evidence as to whether the arsonist knew his way around the factory or not. A window in the office had been broken as a means of access and the offices, wood built, were the obvious place to start a fire. It seemed anyone might have done it. After this experience, Francesca was on tenterhooks, convinced that something more, something even worse, would finally succeed in destroying Lorrimers.

One evening, a month after the fire, at about eight o'clock, there was a hesitant knock on Francesca's front door. It was so quiet she almost didn't hear, but happened to be in the hall on her way to the kitchen at the time.

She opened the door. It was a dark night, pouring with rain, a foul time for anyone to be out and the figure on her doorstep, swathed in dripping headscarf, was soaked.

"Yes?" Francesca could see little more than her outline in the darkness.

"Miss Lorrimer? It's Polly Williams. Do you remember me? My Dad worked at Lorrimers years ago."

"Polly! Why, of course I do! Come in at once, out of the rain!" Francesca stepped back and drew Polly into the hall. She stood on the mat just inside the door, dripping and shivering with the cold.

"Take your coat off and come into the sitting room. I'll get you something hot to drink." Francesca helped her off with her coat, slipped it over the back of a chair in front of the kitchen fire and ushered Polly into the sitting room.

Polly stood in the middle of the floor, twisting her hands nervously. Francesca drew her gently towards the chair nearest the fire and, abandoning the idea of making her a hot drink, poured a small glass of brandy and thrust it into her hands.

"What's wrong, Polly?" she asked. "What on earth has brought you out on a night like this?"

"It's me Dad, Miss Lorrimer." Polly took a gulp of the brandy and choked.

"Your father? He's not ill, is he?" Francesca said in concern.

When she had recovered, Polly said, "No, Miss. Nothing like that. Dad's fit as a flea. Well, in himself he is. But he's been so worried — that mithered I didn't know what to do for the best."

"Tell me all about it," Francesca urged.

"I don't rightly know what's got into him. He goes to the pub on the corner on a Friday night and a week or so ago he came home in a right state. Wanted to come and see you, he said, but it was gone ten o'clock by then and anyway, he can't walk more than fifty yards these days. Never goes further than the pub. He went on about it all week, but there's no buses between our place and

221

yours. He couldn't get to you and he's no good at using one of those public telephones. Said it wasn't something he could say on the telephone anyway. I offered to come and see you myself, but he wouldn't say what it was all about. So at last I said I'd come and ask you — do you think you could come and see him, find out what this is all about? He won't rest, he keeps fussing and worrying and saying he's got to talk to you. I can't put up with it much longer."

"Of course I'll come and see him!" Francesca said at once. "Do you mean now?"

"I'm sorry to give you such bother." Polly said, twisting her hands again in embarrassment. "He gets these ideas in his head — he's getting old. I wouldn't trouble you — I shouldn't have come — "

"Of course you should! I'll get my coat and car keys. I wouldn't let you walk home again in this weather anyway." Francesca got out her car and installed Polly, still apologising, in the passenger seat. Ten minutes later they drew up outside Arthur's little terraced house. Polly scuttled inside.

"Dad!" She called as Francesca followed her into the narrow passage beyond the front door. "Miss Lorrimer's come to see you! So now perhaps you'll stop all this mithering and tell her what you won't tell me."

Francesca found the old man in their tiny living room, hunched over a fire in much the same position as he'd been when she'd come to see him after Frank's death.

"Miss Lorrimer, it's very good of you to come out to see me," he said, clasping her hand and trying to rise from his chair at the same time. She helped him back into it, and sat down opposite him in what was probably Polly's chair. Polly, tactfully, disappeared into the kitchen.

"What was it you wanted to tell me, Arthur?" she asked gently. The man seemed disturbed, his hands continually

223

plucking at the rug over his knees.

"I heard as how you had a fire at the factory a while back," he said finally.

"Yes. Everywhere was a mess and the office was gutted, but the workers were wonderful. They cleared everything up and we're almost back to normal now." Had the news upset the old man, she wondered? He had worked there for so long it must almost seem like a second home.

"Did they find out what caused it?" he asked.

"The investigators said it was arson, deliberately set on fire. But we don't know anything more. The police haven't any idea who could have done it."

"But I know." Arthur spoke so quietly that Francesca wasn't sure she had heard him correctly.

"What do you mean, Arthur?" She put her hands over the old man's, stilling them. In spite of the heat from the fire, they felt cold.

"I go to the Nag's Head on the corner, every Friday night, 'bout half

224

past eight," Arthur said. He gazed into the fire dreamily. "Been going there every Friday now for nigh on fifty years, I reckon."

"Yes?" Francesca prompted.

"Was in there last Friday week an' all. They got an old wooden settle with a high back, old fashioned thing, near the fire. I always sit there if it's vacant." And it probably would be, Francesca thought. The locals would leave it for a customer who'd been coming to the place for fifty years.

"Tucked away, like. High back keeps the draughts off but you can't be seen, neither." He looked at Francesca and his eyes twinkled. "Young chap came in and sat behind me. He was meeting someone, a middle-aged man, well-to-do. I noticed him come in because he wasn't a regular. Didn't look the sort of chap who'd come to a place like the Nag's Head. More your town centre pub type, cocktails and posh drinks like that. He went and sat with the young chap and I heard him say 'You done it, then?' and the chap said, yes, he'd chucked a lot of petrol around but he couldn't get into the machine shop 'cos the door was locked. 'Well, is it burnt down then?' asks the older chap, and the lad said as how the office part was all gone but only the roof of the factory caught light before the fire brigade came. 'Thought it would burn all night,' he said, 'but some interfering so and so saw smoke and called the fire brigade.' Then this older chap kept on about was you going to close down and the young chap said he didn't know. He asked the older man for his payoff, and there was a right old dingdong argument about that, as the man said he hadn't made a proper job of it, but I heard the rustle of notes after a while and it sounded like the young chap was given some money, though from the way he took it, seemed like he thought it wasn't enough. I heard every word, Miss Lorrimer, clear as anything, and they never knew I was there. It's been on my mind ever since, wondering what I should do. I was a right trouble to Polly till she said she'd go and see you and ask you to drop by. It was good of you to come so soon."

"Would you be prepared to tell all this to the police?" Francesca asked. Her voice shook with tension. "You might have to go to court, stand up in a witness box and tell everything to a judge."

"Aye, I'd thought of that. I'd do that, right enough. I'd do anything for Mr Frank and yourself, Miss. And I'd do anything to catch those varmints who are trying to destroy Lorrimers."

"Could you describe both of them, do you think?" She thought of the doctor's vague impression. The police could do nothing if all Arthur had heard were two disembodied voices.

"Describe 'em? Well, I don't know as I recall much what they were wearing." He paused, then said, "But I knew who they both were."

227

"You *knew* them?" Her heart gave a great leap.

"Not to be acquainted, like. The young lad I know because he lives round here. Terry Callaghan he was. Lives in the next street."

"Terry Callaghan! But he's one of my apprentices!" Francesca exclaimed. "He's been with us about six months."

Arthur nodded. "Aye, I know. And before that he worked for Wheelers, the builders. Wheeler wants to get his hands on every bit of open space round Stonebridge and build an estate of houses on it. Got an obsession with developing, he has. Gets his picture in the local paper every six months or so, standing outside some showhouse in a new estate he's just completed. That's how I knew who the other chap was. George Wheeler, Stonebridge's land grabber and jerry builder. 'Spose he thought he'd meet Terry in the Nag's Head where no one would know him. Don't suppose anyone else there did, but I read the local paper every week, cover to cover. Not got much else to do these days. I'm not a great one for books."

"Arthur, I think you're wonderful!" Francesca put her arms round the old man and kissed his cheek impulsively. He looked embarrassed, then a flush of pleasure lit up his face. "I remember when you were a little tot, no more'n five, and you came to the factory with your ma one day. I carried you round and showed you all the machines working — it was safer to carry you so you wouldn't touch anything. Then, when I'd gone all round, you said 'Thank you, Uncle Arthur' and you kissed me on the cheek. I remember that."

Francesca's eyes glistened. "I remember, too," she said. "It was the day I decided I wanted to work at the factory when I grew up. It was your showing me and explaining everything that decided me."

"Like to think so," Arthur said complacently. "You'd best be off,

now. Getting real late. And you tell
the police first thing tomorrow, what
I told you. They can come round and
take a statement from me any time. I
may be old, but I'm not senile and I'm
not deaf, neither."

8

THE police acted quickly, once Francesca told them what Arthur Williams had heard. Terry Callaghan was arrested and promptly confessed, not only to the arson, but to all the other annoying happenings at Lorrimers; the order for Wentworths going astray, the sand in the van's engine, the spanner in the machine. Wheeler, it seemed was desperate to buy the land on which Lorrimers stood. As a one-time airfield, there was plenty of space, but the factory building itself blocked the only access from the road. Frank had bought most of the airfield land with a view to possible future expansion, many years previously.

"You owe Howard Rutherford an apology for thinking he was behind all that," Mavis said, when Francesca told her the whole story. "I don't know how you thought a man in his position would stoop to such things."

"Wheeler owned a big building company," Francesca protested. "He used to write to us every so often asking to buy the land, but Dad always refused. He didn't like the idea of losing so much of our open space around Stonebridge. I suppose Wheeler thought he could get rid of me easily once I was by myself."

"So are you going to telephone Howard? At least tell him what's happened?" Mavis persisted.

"Oh, Mavis, I'd like to! But I can't get away from the fact that he's married, and he flirted with me and behaved as if he wasn't," Francesca said wretchedly.

"Still angry with him? Was it your pride that was hurt, or something more?"

"The trouble with you, Mavis, is that you know me too well," Francesca sighed. "I really thought that Howard and I — well, it doesn't matter now.

He's got a wife and child so I'm steering well clear. I don't intend to be responsible for breaking up a marriage."

Mavis turned back to her new computer terminal. There was no point in discussing Howard Rutherford with Francesca if the man was married. She hoped her friend would soon forget him and regain the sparkle she'd had a few months back. Even the rebuilding of part of Lorrimers, the smart new office block and the foundations of the canteen being dug out behind the machine shop, hadn't seemed to lift Francesca's spirits. The company was doing well now, and with the worry of the last few months behind them, she should be relaxing a bit more, going out to enjoy herself and meet people. Mavis knew that Francesca spent most evenings alone in front of the TV. She still went to view any cottages that came on the market, but so far there hadn't been anything that appealed, nor had there been many enquiries to purchase

Francesca's present home.

"You ought to get out more," she said, glancing across at Francesca, who now had a desk in the larger, open-plan office.

"Why? Where to?" Francesca laughed.

"A girl of your age should have some fun. Look, I know it's not exactly the social event of the year, but come with me to Chris's school concert, will you? He'd be thrilled to bits if you did."

"A primary school concert? Well, at least you can't do much in the way of matchmaking for me, there," Francesca said. "Of course I'll come. I'd love to see Chris in the school concert. What's he doing?"

Mavis giggled. "Playing a triangle. He brought a bit of paper home he said was his musical score. All it said was 'sing, sing, sing,' on it."

They took the afternoon off to go to Chris's school concert. Francesca felt rather out of place at first, among all the young mothers, most of them about her own age, some with a five year old and a second, younger child as well.

They sat on low chairs, grouped in a semi circle, three deep, round the main assembly hall. There was no stage, but the children performed in the centre of the room, most of them without the self-consciousness that develops at a slightly older age. They had a song and a little play, performed by the juniors, the top classes of seven year olds. Then it was the turn of the younger ones, four classes of them, ending with the children who had newly started that term.

Chris marched on with all his classmates, gave them a discreet wave, and played his triangle in all the right places. Francesca and Mavis gave him tremendous applause end he marched off in line, looking very pleased with himself.

The concert ended with a general sing-song from the whole school, in which the audience were invited to join. Being on a midweek afternoon, almost all the parents were mothers, with a scattering of grandfathers and grandmothers who were found more comfortable, adult chairs at the back.

At the end of the concert, Mavis said, "We'll wait and collect him. He won't be long." Francesca looked round at the sea of mothers collecting their offspring and bearing them off home. She didn't exactly envy them, but she did begin to wonder what it would be like to have a small child, to watch proudly as they learnt new skills. To have someone of her very own, to cherish, to bring up, to teach all the things she'd learnt herself from her parents. It didn't look as if that was ever going to happen. Lorrimers was her baby, the only one she'd ever be likely to have. Some women might envy her, a career woman who owned a small but prosperous business, but was that, alone, enough? If she were really honest with herself she had to admit that it wasn't. There was still, at the back of her mind, the thought that she would have liked to have married and had a family. It wasn't possible, of course, because the only person she had ever cared for enough to think of marrying, already had an attractive young wife and a little daughter.

Chris came running up to them, interrupting her thoughts. He was dragging his school coat and his school tie had slipped up under his right ear, but he had a broad grin on his face.

"Did you hear me? I tinged all right, didn't I?" he greeted them.

"You were great, Chris." Francesca dragged her mind back to the present. "How would you like to have tea at MacDonald's to celebrate?"

Chris's eyes lit up. "Yeah, rather! D'you mean now?"

"Yes, why not?"

"Only — I wanted to wait for my friend. She's my bestest friend and she plays the triangle, too."

"We must certainly meet her, then," Mavis said at once. "Where is she? Go and find her and bring her over. Perhaps she'd like to come to

MacDonald's with us."

Christopher dived off into the crowd of children filling the hall, and came back a few moments later, dragging a small girl by the hand.

"This is my friend Cheryl," he announced proudly.

Francesca stared at the child, for a moment not registering why she looked familiar. Then she remembered, and her heart somersaulted. This was the child she had seen in the hall of Howard's house — Howard's daughter!

"Hello," Cheryl said politely. "Did you like our concert?"

"Yes, very much," Francesca stammered.

"Hello, Cheryl. Is your mummy here? We are going to MacDonald's for tea and we wondered if you'd both like to join us," Mavis said, smiling at the little girl.

Oh, no! Francesca groaned. Don't let her mother come with us. I couldn't bear it!

Cheryl was hopping up and down

with excitement. "I'll find mummy and ask her," she said, diving back into the throng of children and parents.

Francesca didn't know what to do. She could hardly spoil everything for Christopher by not taking the little girl. But if her mother came as well, which seemed likely, it would be an impossible situation.

"Look, Mavis. You take them to MacDonald's. I ought to go back to the office — " She thrust some notes into Mavis's hand, adding, "Give Chris a treat from me."

Mavis stared, a hurt expression in her eyes. "But I thought — Fran, there surely isn't any need to get back to the office. I've cleared all the post, and Jim can deal with anything that crops up. I did tell him we wouldn't be back."

"Yes, I know. But I — "

It was too late. Cheryl was back, dragging her mother up to them, the young, attractive woman who was all too familiar to Francesca. There couldn't be any mistake; she was definitely the woman who had answered the door of Howard's house, who had found Howard's bleeper somewhere only a wife would have found it.

"You must be Christopher's mother." The girl smiled at Mavis. "Cheryl said, you had invited her to MacDonald's for tea. I hope she didn't invite herself."

"Of course she didn't. I extended the invitation to both of you," Mavis said. Turning to Francesca, she added, "And you're coming with us. I'm not listening to silly excuses. I bet you've never been to a MacDonald's before. It'll be a new experience for you." To the girl, she said "I'm Mavis, and this is my friend Francesca. I've seen you at the school before but I can't keep calling you Cheryl's mum."

"My name's Gina," the girl smiled back. She looked at Francesca curiously. "Don't I know you? I'm sure I've seen you somewhere."

"I'm not one of the mothers," Francesca said. "I'm Chris's godmother,

240

but I don't have — "

"I know!" Gina broke in. "I saw you a few weeks back! You came round to the house looking for Howard! Did you ever get to find him? According to his secretary he'd gone AWOL and no one knew where he was. Apparently he'd gone off with the company architect and forgot to tell anyone. His mind hasn't been properly on his work for some time now. I think he must be in love."

Francesca felt the blush rising to her cheeks. Did, then, this girl know that Howard dined and wined other women, flirted with them as if he were a single man? And didn't she care?

"Come on, let's be off!" Mavis said gaily, unaware of Francesca's turmoil. She began to usher the two children towards the exit, and Francesca said desperately — "I'm sorry, Mrs Rutherford. You'll have to excuse me. I — I'm feeling rather tired. I have a headache — " She floundered for a plausible excuse, longing to run out of the building and as far away as possible.

"Oh, I'm sorry!" Gina looked sympathetic. "Actually, my name's Taylor, not Rutherford." Then realisation dawned, and she clapped a hand to her mouth and began to giggle.

"Whoops! Did you think I was Howard's wife? Oh, my goodness!"

"But aren't you? I mean, his — er — ?" Francesca stopped, acutely embarrassed.

"Not his anything! Well, not in the way you mean. I suppose you could say I'm his housekeeper, but I'm not really that, although I do keep the place clean and tidy for him. I'm a single parent. I used to work in the offices at Rutherfords and Cheryl's dad was in the factory, but he disappeared as soon as he knew Cheryl was on the way. I lived with my parents but they're getting on and a toddler in the house got too much for them. So Howard said I could have a couple of rooms in his house, in exchange for taking phone

242

calls and looking after the place. It's a super house to live in, but, as he says, it's far too big for just him by himself."

"He's not married, then?" Francesca had to know.

"Lord, no!" Gina looked amazed. "Howard's been too busy taking over the business from his father to think of anything like that. Mind you," she dropped her voice and gave a conspiratorial grin. "I think he might have been thinking about it, a few months back. I'm sure there was someone he was interested in, but it came to nothing. She must have been mad to turn him down. Howard's a smashing chap, but I suppose some women wouldn't be able to cope with someone who's wrapped up in his engineering business."

"Let's go," Mavis interrupted, "before all the other mums have the same idea and we're crowded out. Are you coming, Francesca, or not?"

"Do come, Auntie Fran," Christopher begged.

"Yes, I think, after all, perhaps I will," Francesca replied. "I'm sure it isn't a good thing to be wrapped up in business matters all the time. One misses so much."

It was the following day before Mavis was able to talk to her friend in the privacy of their now shared, office.

"Are you satisfied now that the poor man isn't a two-timing philanderer? I take back all I said about him. Obviously, he did mean exactly what he said; he was interested in you, not acquiring Lorrimers once he knew you didn't plan to sell."

"I feel so ashamed," Francesca said. "He was a really nice man, playing Father Christmas to the children in hospital and never seeking publicity about it, and offering a home to a single parent. And I was so horrible to him!"

"Sounds like it's apology time," Mavis observed.

"But what could I possibly say to him, after the way I've treated him?

Besides, what would he think if I turned up unexpectedly after meeting Gina? I'd feel as if I were throwing myself at him," Francesca protested.

"You could call at his office to thank him for offering us office space after the fire," Mavis suggested. "And you could tell him about Wheeler trying to put you out of business. Now *that* might interest him. Rutherfords covers several acres, so Wheeler might have set his beady eyes on acquiring some of their land, too."

"I hardly think so. Wheeler wouldn't be so crazy. He'll be coming up for trial in a few months and then I imagine he won't be in a position to do any building for some time."

"Don't you think Howard might like to know that?"

"Why should he? He'll read about it in the local paper."

Mavis sighed. "However am I going to get you two together? You heard what Gina said. It's obvious Howard was genuinely interested in you. And

I could see you were very happy while you were seeing him."

"I *can't* go chasing after him. How could I, after the things I said, the way I accused him?"

"You should go on a diet," Mavis snapped unexpectedly. "Large portions of humble pie, my girl. What do you think the poor man must be feeling, if *you're* feeling wretched?"

"I'll think about it," Francesca said, and that was as far as Mavis could persuade her on the subject.

But think about it she did, and a few days later she decided to go and see Howard at Rutherfords. Not, she told herself, with any idea that the relationship might be renewed; that seemed unlikely now, but Mavis had been right and she owed it to the man to apologise for her behaviour. He had been nothing but kind and helpful and he'd not mentioned buying Lorrimers once she'd made it clear she wasn't selling.

Francesca was feeling very nervous

as she drove into the visitors' car park at Rutherfords and walked towards the main entrance. She hadn't telephoned to make an appointment: afraid that she might lose her nerve if she committed herself to a definite time. If Howard wasn't there, or was too busy to see her, she'd go away and drop the idea. But if he could see her, she'd tell him —

What was she going to tell him? She had tried to compose a speech in her head, imagining conversations in which she had explained her reactions to each situation, but the net result only seemed to make her appear suspicious and untrusting. She could just imagine Howard responding with a sarcastic comment which would demolish her completely.

The Receptionist was cool. "If you don't have an appointment it may be difficult. He's a busy man, you know," she admonished in patronising tones. "I'll telephone his office and see what his secretary says."

Fortunately, the secretary remembered

Francesca's name. She asked to speak to her personally and said in a friendly manner, "He's got someone with him at the moment, but there's nothing in the diary afterwards. If you'd like to come up to the office and wait, you'll probably be able to catch him before he goes home."

Francesca thanked her and took the lift to the top floor, where Howard had a suite of offices.

Roz Chapman greeted her and offered a seat in a comfortable armchair in the outer office, plus coffee, which Francesca refused.

The door connecting with Howard's office was slightly open. She could hear voices coming from within, but not what was being said.

"He shouldn't be too long," Roz reassured her. "But it's a friend of his so they sometimes go on chatting after the official business. Would you like me to tell him you're here?"

"No, thank you. I'll take my chance whether he has time to see me.

This isn't a business visit," Francesca replied.

Five minutes later Roz took a telephone call at her desk. Putting down the receiver, she said, "Please excuse me, Miss Lorrimer. I'm wanted at the other end of the building. If Mr Rutherford's guest goes before I'm back, do go in and let him know you're here, will you? I'm sorry to have to leave, but it's a query only this office can sort out. I shouldn't be too long."

Francesca barely glanced at the magazines Roz had left beside her. Her courage was beginning to desert her. How could she even begin to explain to Howard that she'd believed him to be a married man?

She got up and strolled nervously round the room. She hadn't meant to eavesdrop, hadn't even paid any attention to the inaudible murmur coming from the main office, but as she passed the door she heard, distinctly, the name 'Lorrimers'.

She had to stop. She couldn't help herself. It was Howard's voice, but it was the other speaker who had mentioned her name.

"Oh, yes, I know the Lorrimer company," Howard was saying. "It's a very small outfit, compared to Rutherfords but I believe they have plans to expand in the near future."

Howard's companion asked what was evidently a question. Howard's voice came to her clearly. "Certainly! Very sound. I know Miss Lorrimer well. She's an extraordinarily competent businesswoman. Don't let her apparent youth put you off. She's good. And that company of hers — you can rest assured that if you continue to invest in it your capital will be perfectly safe. I'd have liked to have had her come and work with me, a partnership with Rutherfords, but she's an independent young woman and prefers to go her own way."

Again his companion said something which Francesca didn't catch, but

Howard, who must have been facing the door or nearer to it, laughed and said "Yes, and beautiful, too! Naturally, I had a personal motive for wanting her to come and work with me. What man wouldn't? But she was wedded to her career. I did my best but evidently she wasn't interested in me."

Francesca's cheeks flamed. She realised that she had been standing just outside the door. Who said eavesdroppers never heard any good about themselves? Quickly she stepped away, and heard the scrape of chairs as Howard and his visitor stood up. They would be coming out any minute and they mustn't find her here, clearly having heard their conversation.

She crossed to the outer door and slipped through it into the passage. She'd have to make some excuse and leave, but how was she going to stop them telling Howard she'd been waiting to see him?

When the lift deposited her on the ground floor she saw that the

Receptionist was busy signing for special delivery parcels. Quickly, she slipped past without being noticed and ran towards her car. The keys were in her jacket pocket so it wasn't until she sat down in the driving seat that she realised she had left her handbag upstairs in the chair in the outer office.

Impossible to go back there now. She'd have to leave it and telephone Howard's secretary tomorrow and arrange to collect it from Reception. With luck, Howard needn't know about it. She had her house keys on the same ring with the car, so there was no problem until tomorrow. She could do without money for the rest of the day.

She was still shaky from the effects of what she'd heard. Did Howard really consider her such a good businesswoman? She'd never thought he'd consider any woman capable of being good in a business capacity. But then, she'd been wrong about him on so many counts.

She pushed her key into the ignition but before she could turn it, she heard an urgent tapping on the window beside her. Looking up, she saw Howard, holding up her handbag and gesticulating to her to wind down the window.

"Isn't this your handbag? I thought I recognised it and then I saw your car from the office window." He sounded slightly out of breath.

"Yes, it is mine," she admitted unwillingly. "I'm sorry, I couldn't wait."

He gave her a shrewd glance but made no attempt to hand over her handbag. "That's a pity," he said. "Otherwise you might have overheard even more flattering comments about yourself."

Her cheeks burned scarlet again. "I didn't deliberately eavesdrop," she said, then, to cover her embarrassment, added, "I suppose the remarks I did hear were deliberately intended for me. You knew I was in the outer office."

Howard looked surprised. "No, I didn't. I didn't know you were anywhere around until I came out of my office and saw your handbag on the chair. My secretary came back and confirmed she'd left you waiting to see me. You didn't have to rush away. If I'd known you were there I'd have introduced you to my visitor, Giles Bannister. He told me he'd invested in Lorrimers and asked my opinion. He'd have liked to have met you and you should have met him, if he was one of your investors."

"Mr Anderson said he wanted to remain anonymous. I thought it was you."

Howard raised his eyebrows. "Me? Why should I want — Oh, I see! You thought it was some subtle way of getting my hands on your factory, I suppose."

"I'm sorry. I did you an injustice there." She couldn't meet his eyes, but he persisted. "What did you come to see me about? Look, I can't keep standing here bending down to talk through your window. Either come back to my office or open your passenger door and let me sit inside."

She reached across and unlocked the door. Howard came round and sat beside her, tossing her handbag on to the back seat.

"Now, what is it, Francesca?" He turned to face her.

"I met Gina Taylor the other day," she began.

Howard gave a quiet chuckle. "And you thought she was my live-in girlfriend, or mistress, or even worse? What a rake you must think I am, or can you never believe I could ever do my own washing up?"

"I'm sorry. But I went to your house to ask your advice about all the trouble we were having at Lorrimers, and to thank you for lending us the van. Gina opened the door, with Cheryl. What was I to think?"

Howard's chuckle became a full, deep laugh. "And so you jumped to the wrong conclusion! Just because

I share a part of my large home with a girl who has had a rough deal and nowhere to live! For your information, in lieu of rent she does my washing up, and my cleaning, and makes my bed, but she doesn't share it. I give you my word, Gina does no more than share my home; not my life."

"I realised that when I met her at Christopher's school concert," Francesca said. "I came to see you today to apologise for what I'd thought, and for all the other things I'd accused you of."

"I think I'd sooner not know what they are," Howard said. "But I can guess. Trying to steal your company; trying to burn it down, trying to put you out of business so that I could buy it cheaply; trying to seduce you while keeping a secret girlfriend and love child in my home — "

"Oh, don't!" Francesca was near tears.

"I was teasing. But now, looking at

you, I'm beginning to wonder if it wasn't all true. You *did* think that badly of me. Why do you dislike me so much, Francesca?"

She couldn't answer. She merely shook her head.

"You heard for yourself what I think of you. And that was true; I didn't know you were there to hear."

"I thought — "

"You thought a lot of daft things, because you didn't have the confidence to believe in yourself. Now, tell me. Didn't you have doubts about managing Lorrimers on your own?"

She nodded.

"Well, I didn't. As soon as I'd come to know you, I knew you could do it, if you only had a little help and encouragement. But you had doubts about me, too, because you wouldn't believe me when I told you you were becoming important to me. I meant it, you know."

Her hands were gripping the steering wheel. Gently he prised them off and took them in his own. "I still mean it," he said. "Can't we begin again? Or is that quite out of the question?"

She wanted to look at him, but his gentleness was her undoing. He had to take her chin in his fingers and turn her face towards him.

"You've no idea how lonely I've been," he said. "When I met you I thought that here at last was someone with whom I could share my life, someone who would truly understand my work and my life. I hoped you might feel the same way."

She reacted then. "I do!" She whispered with a sob, and put her arms round his neck.

"Fran, my love, my darling. I am going to kiss you now, and after that you'll never be able to change your mind about me. In twenty seconds the entire Rutherfords staff will be pouring out at the end of the shift to see their Managing Director kissing Lorrimer's boss in the car park. Rumours of a merger are bound to be rife."

"And I shan't mind a bit!" she said, kissing him back as the factory hooter blared out.

THE END

WITH SOMEBODY ELSE
Theresa Charles

Rosamond sets off for Cornwall with Hugo to meet his family, blissfully unaware of the shocks in store for her.

A SUMMER FOR STRANGERS
Claire Hamilton

Because she had lost her job, her flat and she had no money, Tabitha agreed to pose as Adam's future wife although she believed the scheme to be deceitful and cruel.

VILLA OF SINGING WATER
Angela Petron

The disquieting incidents that occurred at the Vatican and the Colosseum did not trouble Jan at first, but then they became increasingly unpleasant and alarming.

DOCTOR NAPIER'S NURSE
Pauline Ash

When cousins Midge and Derry are entered as probationer nurses on the same day but at different hospitals they agree to exchange identities.

A GIRL LIKE JULIE
Louise Ellis

Caroline absolutely adored Hugh Barrington, but then Julie Crane came into their lives. Julie was the kind of girl who attracts men without even trying.

COUNTRY DOCTOR
Paula Lindsay

When Evan Richmond bought a practice in a remote country village he did not realise that a casual encounter would lead to the loss of his heart.

ENCORE
Helga Moray

Craig and Janet realise that their true happiness lies with each other, but it is only under traumatic circumstances that they can be reunited.

NICOLETTE
Ivy Preston

When Grant Alston came back into her life, Nicolette was faced with a dilemma. Should she follow the path of duty or the path of love?

THE GOLDEN PUMA
Margaret Way

Catherine's time was spent looking after her father's Queensland farm. But what life was there without David, who wasn't interested in her?

HOSPITAL BY THE LAKE
Anne Durham

Nurse Marguerite Ingleby was always ready to become personally involved with her patients, to the despair of Brian Field, the Senior Surgical Registrar, who loved her.

VALLEY OF CONFLICT
David Farrell

Isolated in a hostel in the French Alps, Ann Russell sees her fiancé being seduced by a young girl. Then comes the avalanche that imperils their lives.

NURSE'S CHOICE
Peggy Gaddis

A proposal of marriage from the incredibly handsome and wealthy Reagan was enough to upset any girl — and Brooke Martin was no exception.

A DANGEROUS MAN
Anne Goring

Photographer Polly Burton was on safari in Mombasa when she met enigmatic Leon Hammond. But unpredictability was the name of the game where Leon was concerned.

PRECIOUS INHERITANCE
Joan Moules

Karen's new life working for an authoress took her from Sussex to a foreign airstrip and a kidnapping; to a real life adventure as gripping as any in the books she typed.

VISION OF LOVE
Grace Richmond

When Kathy takes over the rundown country kennels she finds Alec Stinton, a local vet, very helpful. But their friendship arouses bitter jealousy and a tragedy seems inevitable.

CRUSADING NURSE
Jane Converse

It was handsome Dr. Corbett who opened Nurse Susan Leighton's eyes and who set her off on a lonely crusade against some powerful enemies and a shattering struggle against the man she loved.

WILD ENCHANTMENT
Christina Green

Rowan's agreeable new boss had a dream of creating a famous perfume using her precious Silverstar, but Rowan's plans were very different.

DESERT ROMANCE
Irene Ord

Sally agrees to take her sister Pam's place as La Chartreuse the dancer, but she finds out there is more to it than dyeing her hair red and looking like her sister.